Cake in Bed

By Sheri Fink

Contemporary Romance • Women's Fiction
Cake in Bed

The Whimsical World of Sheri Fink Children's Books
The Little Rose
The Little Gnome
The Little Firefly
The Little Seahorse
Exploring the Garden with the Little Rose

Personal Development • Self-Help
My Bliss Book

Cake in Bed

Sheri Fink

LOVE · BLISS · INSPIRATION

Library of Congress Control Number: 2015921090

Print Edition
ISBN-10: 0-9864468-1-5
ISBN-13: 978-0-9864468-1-8
$15.95

eFormat Edition
ISBN-10:0-9864468-2-3
ISBN-13:978-0-9864468-2-5
$9.95

Editor: Michelle Josette
http://www.mjbookeditor.com
Cover Design: Kelsey at **K Keeton Designs**

To love, laughter, and happily ever after.

One

Julie sits in bed, alone, wearing her disheveled old wedding dress, eating what would have been her frozen anniversary cake, and crying while listening to "Wedding Dress" by Matt Nathanson on repeat.

Happily ever after is so once upon a time—more fairytale than reality.

Julie has the music turned up so loud that she barely hears Nick knock on the door. He walks in and looks at her, a crumpled mess.

"Oh, Julie. I'm sorry you're going through this. You know you did the right thing."

She just shrugs and bites off another mouthful of cake.

He looks closer. "Oh, you're wearing *the dress*," he says, trying, not-so-subtly, to cover how shocked he is.

"I know. It's bad, right?" She gasps to catch her breath. "I don't know what to do. I can't take it off." Her eyes plead him not to judge her.

Nick gives her his best sympathetic look. "Okay. It's okay." He scoots into bed next to her and holds her hand against his chest, which only makes her sob harder as she leans into him. When she finally lifts her head up to look at him, she notices frosting from the side of her face smeared on his shirt. She laughs, then wipes it off with a finger and licks it up.

"Buttercream definitely doesn't get better with time," she says, and Nick chuckles.

"How do I cheer you up?" he asks. Another shrug. The lightness she'd felt a moment ago has already left.

He holds her tighter in his strong arms, where she feels safe. She trusts him completely.

Nathanson continues to croon in the background, the lyrics tugging at her.

"I'm sorry, Nick. I feel so weak. I'm such a mess right now."

He shakes his head. "Don't ever apologize for how you feel. There's beauty in your fragility. It's okay to be exactly as you are, big emotions and all. You're very special, and the right man will recognize that and never be crazy enough to let you go. I'm sure of it, and I'm here for you."

She nods, disbelieving.

"I'm serious," Nick says. "I'll always be here."

"No, I know that. It's the other part I'm not so sure of." She lays her head back on his chest, still sobbing but somewhat soothed by the rhythm of his breathing.

"Are you comfortable in this?" he asks, touching her ruffled skirt.

Her cheeks warm as she looks up at him again. "Not really," she says. "I feel ridiculous."

"Well, let's get you out of that thing." Nick gives her a wink and stands.

She sits up and takes his hand as he pulls her out of bed. She leans against him again, her legs unsteady. "I don't know if I can stand up right now, Nick."

"It's okay. Just lean against my chest. I can support you. Do you need help?"

"That would be wonderful." She sighs, and leans her full weight on him as he slowly and carefully unties the corset-style ribbon crisscrossing the back of her gown. She feels the ribbon unraveling before remembering that she's naked under the dress.

"Nick," she quickly whispers, "close your eyes." He nods, allowing her to step out of the giant creampuff that now gathers on the floor.

She stumbles toward the carpet as she pulls herself free of the dress. Instinctively, Nick opens his eyes and moves to catch her.

"Don't look!" she pleads.

"I'm sorry, Julie. I accidentally looked for a second when I heard you falling. I have my eyes closed again now."

The song climaxes in the background. Her face flushes with embarrassment, but she's too emotionally exhausted to care. Here Nick is, seeing her at her most vulnerable point, but she's happy to have him with her.

Nick breaks the awkward silence that follows. "For what it's worth, I only had a quick peek, and you have one of the most beautiful bodies I've ever seen . . . cake and all."

She laughs, though she still feels kind of silly.

"Can I get you something to put on so I can open my eyes?" he asks. "How about some pajamas?"

"Okay, that sounds good. Top middle drawer."

With eyes still closed, Nick leads her to sit on the bed, and then he turns away to get her nightgown. He opens the drawer and freezes.

"Sorry about those," she says, cringing slightly. She knew he'd found her nightshirt next to a whole stack of sexy, lacy panties.

"Your ex-husband is a crazy man, Julie." Nick grabs the shirt that playfully says 'Come back to bed' and hands it to her without turning around.

She pulls the soft cotton nightgown over her body and crawls under the covers.

"Is it safe to turn around now?" he asks.

"Yes. Thank you, Nick." When he turns to face her, she can't help quietly start to cry again. Nick comes over and wraps his arms around her, placing sweet little kisses across her forehead as she snuggles into him.

"Everything is going to be fine," he says. "No. Better than fine."

"I don't understand how this could happen to me. I did everything I could think of to make his life good."

"It's not about you. You're amazing, and he's not worthy of you. You didn't do anything wrong. I'm proud of you."

Nick is almost convincing. His voice calms her, but she still hurts. Her mascara dries in puddles around her eyes and in perma-teardrops down her cheeks.

"I know today would've been one year," Nick says. "I promise it'll get easier with time."

Her tears soak through his shirt and drip onto his skin, one at a time, before they start rolling faster.

"What else can I do to help you, Julie?"

"Just hold me."

She cries herself to sleep on his chest, feeling hot tears rolling into her ear and burning as they evaporate, the smell of stale buttercream in her hair.

Nick rubs her arms and strokes her hair before drifting away into his own ocean of thoughts. Caught somewhere between half-asleep and half-awake, she feels his light kisses linger against her forehead before he closes his eyes to rest with her. He is her best friend, and his presence alone calms her. Right now she needs him as much as she ever has.

As sleep finally comes, a shiver rolls through her body and Nick pulls the blanket up to cover them both. He whispers into her ear, "You are so special, Julie. Please don't let any man treat you like you don't matter. Sweet dreams."

And for the first time in months, she feels at peace.

Two

Enveloped in her fleece blanket, Julie awakens to the smell and sizzle of eggs cooking. Still bleary-eyed, she glances around the room. *What time is it? What day is it?* She looks down at the enormous pile of toile on the floor beside her bed. *Yep, that's my wedding dress. What the hell happened last night?*

Nick pops his head into her bedroom. "Good morning!" he says cheerfully. Last night starts to creep back into her mind—she was such a wreck. She can feel the warmth of embarrassment tinting her cheeks bright pink.

"I got hungry and thought you might like to eat something other than cake," Nick says matter-of-factly. He raises his eyebrows and flashes a grin.

"You didn't have to do that, Nick."

"I know. I wanted to." He lifts up a freshly squeezed juice and brings a huge plate of eggs over to the bed for her. He reaches down to the floor and gathers pillows to support her back, then nestles in next to her above the covers.

"*Bon appétit.*"

Her stomach grumbles loudly and she eagerly digs in. She hasn't had the energy to do any cooking for a week, any *anything*, and she's just now realizing how hungry she is.

"You know one of the things I love about your place?" Nick asks playfully. "That you get to eat every meal in bed."

Julie looks up from her plate and smiles. "That's because there's no room to eat anywhere else."

"Well, I like it." They both chuckle.

"How are you feeling?" Nick asks, watching her eat.

In between bites, she tells him, "Like I'm hung over and never want to see that dress or that cake—or that man—again."

Nick laughs. "It's okay. Do you want me to 'dispose' of it for you . . . you know, hide the evidence?" he asks slyly, his bright blue eyes gleaming.

"That would be amazing." She smiles after finishing her last bite and rests her head against him for a moment. "Thank you for being such an incredible friend to me through everything."

"My pleasure, Julie. I love you and I'm always here. You're my best friend." He gathers the empty plates and takes them into the kitchen.

Alone in bed again, she savors the calm as it washes over her, though that feeling of dread, of loss, still settles like a stone in the pit of her stomach. She tries to ignore it. Her belly is full of delicious food, and she's got the best friend a girl could ask for.

Nick returns moments later, slipping his arms through a jacket. "I have to go now to meet Allison, but I'll give you a call later today to check on you. Don't worry, the right man will find you and never let you go. Keep smiling."

He kisses her on the cheek, picks up the white fluffy mound, and leaves.

Later that day, Julie finally builds up the strength to get dressed and go out for the first time in a week. If she didn't, she wouldn't have anything to eat tomorrow, so she talks herself into it even though she's still a mess. After crying in the gym, the grocery store, and the market, she thinks she's pretty much desensitized herself from people's stares and looks of pity. Sadly, she's becoming an expert at crying in public.

On her way home from the market, she feels her phone buzz in her pocket.

"Hi Jolene," she answers.

"Hey girl! What are you doing this weekend? Wanna get together?"

She can't match Jolene's enthusiasm, but she tries her best. "Going to a writers' conference. I'm speaking on Sunday."

"Fun!" Jolene says excitedly. "Maybe you'll meet someone!"

"Haha . . . Not likely. I'm not ready for that, anyway. I'm just trying to put my life back together right now. I don't even feel like going."

Jolene hesitates. "Julie, it's been long enough," she says. "You should just get out there again."

"I'm in no rush. It'll be nice when it happens, but I'm too emotional these days."

Sheri Fink

"You know, you've been single ever since I met you," Jolene chides. "Hey, remember that amazing concert last year?"

"Yeah, I know, it was the night that guy stood me up."

"And good thing because that's how we met! See, good things come from going out on dates . . . even when the date doesn't go the way you thought it would."

Julie feels sick remembering the way things unfolded that night and thinking about her cluelessness when it comes to men, but she knows Jolene has her best interests at heart. "Okay, I promise to be open-minded," she reluctantly agrees.

In a singsong voice, Jolene replies, "Well, have fun! You never know who you may meet . . . maybe someone who wants to hire you, or marry you, or both!"

Julie laughs. "I know, I know. Thanks, Jolene."

"What are friends for?" Jolene says. "I'll see you next week!"

"Okay, see you then!"

Three

Sunday afternoon, Julie walks tall and confident after delivering a successful talk. It's been a full day at the writers' conference, a great distraction, and she is buzzing with the high that comes from doing what she loves. She's worked hard in her career, and the bright-eyed expressions of her fellow writers as she speaks on stage make it all worth it.

She passes the swanky hotel lobby bar as a fellow writer and fan comes running up to her. "Oh my God, Julie!" she gushes. "Your presentation was so awesome! Everyone's talking about it!"

"Oh wow, thank you," Julie says graciously.

"Seriously, I'm totally inspired. I want to treat you to dinner."

"Oh," she says, shaking her head politely, suddenly feeling the ache in her feet from the long day. "No thank you, I'm just exhausted."

"But we should celebrate your successful day! Maybe just a quick drink?" She looks so excited and determined. Julie wouldn't feel right bursting her bubble by saying no.

Reluctantly, she agrees. Maybe it would be nice to celebrate with a glass of champagne.

They step inside and take a seat at the mahogany bar, and Julie immediately begins to feel out of place. She's never been comfortable in bar-type settings, which to her are places full of boring conversations, fake smiles, and people trying too hard.

She gets the attention of the bartender. "I'll have a glass of champagne, please."

Her new friend has suddenly disappeared, and she's alone . . . at the bar, exactly where she didn't want to be. *Where did she go? Why did I agree to this? How long does it take to pour a glass of champagne?* She starts to feel a familiar pang in her stomach. Maybe it's hunger? No, definitely loneliness.

While she waits, her eyes wander over to a handsome man at end of the bar near the red-velvet curtained wall. He stands up and digs in his pocket. She watches as he puts two dollars on the bar, and then seems to change his mind as he picks one bill up, crumples it, and puts it back in his pocket.

How odd. Then, he walks away from the bar and makes eye contact with her. He changes trajectory and navigates his way to her through the crowded bar.

Oh no, he's coming over. I'm not ready. She turns to look at the bartender to pretend she doesn't see him. *Too late.*

"Hi Julie . . ." He smiles slyly. "I saw your talk today. You rocked it!"

She turns to look at him. "Hi, and thanks."

"I'm Evan Waverly." He pushes his hand out and grabs hers. His hand is cold and wet, and he holds on just a little too long.

"Nice to meet you." Julie smiles politely. Looking into his big brown eyes, she forgets momentarily about his clammy handshake and strange introduction.

Her champagne arrives and, distracted, she fumbles with her wallet. "I got it," Evan says and pulls a crinkled $10 bill from his pocket. He makes a grand gesture and slaps it down on the bar with a proud smile.

"Wow . . . you are really beautiful," he says.

She feels her cheeks turn crimson. "Thank you," she quietly responds while sipping champagne. It's been a long time since she's welcomed any attention from a man. Something about Evan draws her in, makes her feel curious. Maybe his awkwardness is endearing. Maybe it's those eyes . . .

No.

"I would love to pick your brain sometime," he tells her. "You know, I'm a writer, too."

It's too bad, this was just starting to get interesting. Ugh . . . I hate when guys pull that line. Cringing inwardly, she reaches into her purse and hands him her business card. "Here you go. Well, have a nice night." She picks up her champagne and walks away.

"Wait—how about dinner tonight?" he shouts out behind her.

She turns and smiles. "No thank you. I have plans."

Leaving the bar, she goes back to her hotel room and spends the night the way she spends most evenings after her events—taking a luxurious bubble bath and ordering room service, for one.

While working out at the gym a few days after the conference, Julie hears the happy tweet of a text message and sees it's from a number she doesn't recognize. She pauses the treadmill and picks up her phone.

"Hi Jules!" the message gleams on the small screen.

She lets out an irritated sigh and types back, "My name is Julie. Who is this?"

"Evan," the next message says.

"Evan who?"

"Evan from the writers' conference. U know, the devastatingly handsome man. We met in the bar."

"Oh, hello," she replies, rolling her eyes.

"I was thinking u should go out w me."

"No thanks, I'm not really dating right now."

"I'd like 2 change that."

So cheesy, she thinks. Still, she can't help but smile upon reading his text. Without further thought, she sets her phone back down and resumes her workout. She feels a little rush of excitement receiving texts from a good-looking guy after being alone for so long.

A few days later, Evan calls at 11:45 p.m. "Hello?" she answers. *What could he be calling about this late?*

"Hey there. What are you doing?"

"I'm getting ready for bed. Why are you calling me so late?"

Evan purrs, "I was just thinking about you. Couldn't get you out of my mind so I decided to give you a call."

"Why are you whispering?"

"Oh, I uh . . ."

"Where are you calling from?" she asks.

"Home."

Julie pauses as things start to make sense. "Is someone else there?"

Evan hesitates. "Well . . . sorta," he says.

"I'm confused. Who's there and why are you whispering?"

"Um . . . it's my girlfriend."

"What?!"

"It's complicated. When I saw you at the conference, I just knew I needed to see you again."

"But you have a girlfriend, Evan." *What in the world is he thinking?*

"Well, yes and no. She hasn't lived here for long and we haven't talked about being exclusive."

Is this guy for real? "You just told me that you live together. That's . . . weird. Goodnight, Evan," she tells him firmly, and hangs up.

Four

A few weeks later, Julie is out running errands. She decides to treat herself to dinner at the local fish shop. While waiting for her food to arrive, she glances down at her phone to see another text from Evan. *Really?* It reads, "Hello stranger." *I should've blocked him after that bizarre phone call.* She looks up and to her shock, sitting right there at the table in front of her is Evan.

"Evan! What are you doing here?"

"Probably the same thing you're doing," he says, smirking as he puts his elbows on the table and rests his head in his hands.

"How's your girlfriend?" she asks with a smile.

The waiter brings her food to the table.

"Well, we broke up," Evan says with a shrug.

"Really? I'm sorry to hear that," she tells him, still startled by Evan's sudden appearance. "When did she move out?"

"Oh, well we're still living together, but we're just friends." His fingers tap anxiously on the wooden table.

"Mmmhmm," she says while digging into her fish and chips.

"So, I was thinking we should hang out," says Evan matter-of-factly.

"I told you, Evan. I'm not dating right now."

"How about just one date and then if you want me to, I'll leave you alone?" He raises his eyebrows a few times.

"And if I don't say yes?"

"I'll keep bugging you until you do."

Ugh. Feeling exasperated and somehow a little flattered, she remembers Jolene daring her to go out with the first guy who asks her. Jolene has a crazy theory that Julie is hiding from romance, that she needs to put herself out there. *Fine!* she thought.

"Okay," she says slowly, "just one date."

The following night, Julie paces around her tiny apartment. She hums quietly to herself as she picks out her earrings and pulls on her black stockings. *Dating . . . I can totally do this.* Yet there's another feeling, a faint cautiousness, stopping her from becoming too excited. She realizes she's nervous about spending time with a man who manipulated her into going on a date with him. And who slightly stalked her at a restaurant.

As she fixes her hair in the mirror, she recalls conversations with Evan and feels a strange mixture of disgust, compassion, and curiosity about him.

She pushes those thoughts aside for the moment and focuses on curling her hair. As a writer who works from home and cafés most of the time, her hair is almost always in a ponytail or tucked under a baseball cap. Tonight, she lets it down and admires the improvement.

She can't help but return to wondering why she's even going on this date with Evan. On the one hand, she likes that he wants to be with her so badly that he's willing to embarrass himself. Then again, now that she thinks about it, he never actually seems embarrassed.

On the other hand, what kind of guy asks a girl out while he's still seeing his live-in girlfriend? She's not sure how she feels about that, but it's registering low on the "morals" scale. And it's definitely *not* sexy.

She feels a little ashamed that she let him beg her into saying yes when she really didn't want to go out with him. She hasn't even told Nick about the conversation or that they have a date—she's that embarrassed. Not that Evan isn't good-looking, and he doesn't seem like a complete asshole. He's actually attractive and appears to be successful from the outside. It's what's inside that concerns her.

The last time she went on a date that the guy actually showed up to, it was a disaster. No connection, no manners, and no goodnight kiss. She remembers wishing she was at home in her pajamas the whole time. *Dating is scary,* she muses, *but it's better than the alternative of ending up alone.*

Well, I guess this will be a learning experience . . . and it's just one date. She consoles herself in the mirror, applying a final coat of lipstick before grabbing her purse and heading out.

Following an unremarkable dinner at a casual Italian restaurant, Evan awkwardly leans in to kiss Julie in the car. It's her first kiss in months and, even though it's not mind-blowing, it's fun.

Wow. It's been a long time since I've been kissed. I didn't realize how much I missed it until this moment.

She longs for more kissing, more closeness. "I want to kiss some more," she says, almost embarrassed that she craves kisses so badly. Evan seems surprised and turned-on by her declaration as he leans in again, this time with his hand on the back of her head, pulling her closer.

"Do you want to go down to the beach?" he asks sheepishly.

Forgetting about the chill in the night air, she acquiesces.

Evan smiles and grabs her hand, leading her down to the sand. The moon is bright tonight and the sky is black surrounding it. He takes her close to the water and sits on the sand. She settles in next to him and they kiss. The kissing gets hotter and more passionate.

He's a little wild, and she likes that. The next thing she knows, they're lying down in the sand with their arms and legs wrapped around each other. She's never moved this fast with anyone before, but she's enjoying the kissing so much that she decides to go with the flow.

She feels his weight as he shifts to lie on top of her, holding her hands down in the sand as he kisses her deeply. "I can feel your passion for me when you kiss me," he says between kisses. "I love the way you kiss. How do you like to be kissed?"

She smiles playfully. "By you," she declares, and rolls over on top of him, straddling him. "Whoa . . . I like that you just took charge and decided to be on top. You look good up there."

She looks down at his face illuminated by the soft glow of the moon. She feels so alive in this moment, wiggling her toes in the cool sand and feeling Evan's solid body beneath her. The closest she's gotten to this feeling of euphoria is when she's in the flow with her writing, although those moments have been rare for the past year. This new feeling of passion is intense and intoxicating. She wants to drink up every moment.

Julie can't help but move her body while kissing him. Everything feels so good. It's been so long since she's been this close, this sexual with a man.

"I want you to be my girlfriend," Evan blurts out suddenly. "I want to see you when you're happy, sad, and frustrated."

She smiles and stares into the moon reflecting in his big brown eyes. She kisses him harder and more intensely than before. *This is kind of fun.*

"I want to travel with you and see where you grew up. I want to know everything about you." His hands caress her back and trace the sides of her butt before she redirects them.

He looks up at her lovingly and says, "When we have sex, I want to be making love to you. We'll get there. We're already going that direction."

She feels his firm manhood between her legs as he gently thrusts her. *I wonder what he's like in bed?* Suddenly she wants to fast-forward to that moment and to slow down at the same time.

He kisses her again and plays with her tongue. "You're the most beautiful woman I've ever seen. I don't know what I did to get this lucky to be with you."

She keeps kissing him. Evan declares, "I'm taking my online dating profile down." She looks up at him. "I know what I want and I've found her."

They kiss and grind some more. Julie begins to become more aware of the cold sand against her hands and feet, but Evan barely seems to notice. She thinks at times that he's moving too fast, but it's been a long time since she's been in the dating world . . . *Maybe this is how things work nowadays?*

She looks up at the sky and he rolls alongside her. With his arms wrapped around her, they watch the clouds blow quickly over the shimmering surface of the moon. The ocean is loud, and the waves crash powerfully against the shore.

As a gust of wind whistles across the ocean, she says, "I think we should leave now."

"Okay, after one more kiss."

She feels so happy to be making out in the moonlight. It feels daring and adventurous and very romantic despite her shivers.

Evan walks her to her car and gives her one more passionate kiss up against the passenger door. She feels a little uncomfortable with being pushed so tightly against the metallic, dirty car door and about the scene he's making in front of all of the teenagers nearby. But the kissing feels so good.

When they get back to his place, he squeezes her thigh with his hand and asks alluringly, "Wanna come inside?"

Much to her surprise, she actually feels tempted. "No, I'm going home now. Thanks for an interesting evening."

He says, "Goodnight, dream girl," and opens the car door. They kiss once more and she gets back into the driver's seat.

She drives home floating on a cloud.

Five

Just another typical hot Friday night . . . me against the blank page. The next night Julie is sitting alone in her tiny apartment trying to write her novel. Suddenly everything else seems to call her and her short attention span away from her work. She feels compelled to clean out her car, do the dishes, scrub the floors, fold her laundry, and even work a puzzle before she can get into her writing. *Why is this so hard?*

Just as she's made up her mind to glue herself to the chair and make progress on her manuscript no matter what, her personal pep talk is interrupted by the tweet of her phone.

She resolves not to answer it. *But maybe it's Evan?* Her pulse quickens as she remembers their hot make-out session on the beach. Curiosity gets the best of her. She takes a quick glance at the screen and sees Nick's face.

"Hey Julie! Wanna join me and Allison for movie night?"

Really wanting to go, she checks the time. It's 5:35 p.m. Then she checks her word count: 14,579.

She texts back, "Would love to! But I gotta make my word count before I leave. What time?"

He answers immediately, "Does 7:30 work for you? Let me know & I'll have dinner ready when you get here."

She smiles. "See you at 7:30! What can I bring?"

"Just yourself. ☺"

Julie decides to get focused and finish strong in her writing. Excited for the evening plans with Nick and his girlfriend, she writes 600 words over her target and then happily packs it up for the night.

Upon arriving at Nick's place, Julie gives her signature knock on the door. Nick swings the door open and greets her with a big hug. "Julie! So glad you could join us tonight!"

She hands him a bottle of his favorite wine.

"Thank you! You really didn't have to bring anything . . ." he says with a grateful smile.

"I know . . . but I saw this and felt like you should have it." She winks at him as she walks into the kitchen to say hi to Allison.

Allison is on the phone having an argument with what seems to be a client. Julie waves at her and she waves back distractedly. Julie immediately goes back to Nick. "So, how are you?"

"Pretty good. Business is going well and things are okay with her." He motions to where Allison is sitting in the other room. "What's new with you?"

"Well, I had a date last night," she says with a coy smile.

"What? That's great! Who's the lucky guy?"

"Do you remember Evan, the one I met at the writers' conference?" She looks down at the floor.

Nick thinks for a moment as he uncorks the wine she brought. "The one with the girlfriend?"

"Yeah, but they're not together anymore. And it wasn't a big deal date or anything."

He raises an eyebrow as he pours three glasses of wine, handing her the first one. "How was it?"

"I wasn't sure at first. I didn't feel that attracted to him, but then he really opened up to me and I had a good time." She smiles with a shrug.

He raises his glass to clink hers and says, "That's great! Have you heard from him today?"

"Um . . . no. But we made out last night. He said he wants me to be his girlfriend and that he's taking down his online dating profile."

Nick nods slowly. They hear Allison's voice get louder on the phone in the other room and move out onto the back porch.

"I don't know about this guy, Julie," he admits. "He sounds like trouble. Go slow, and make sure you really want to date him exclusively."

Just then, Allison bursts out onto the patio, still on the phone and sounding angry. Nick just looks at her, and he motions to Julie to follow him inside and closes the door behind them.

Once inside, he asks if she's hungry.

"Yes!"

"Let's go ahead and eat. She's been on the phone since you got here, and dinner is getting cold."

He pulls out a set of plates and removes a homemade pizza from the oven. The kitchen fills with the delicious smell of baked bread and melted cheese. "This pizza has a whole-wheat crust, regular cheese, and veggies."

Julie's mouth waters as she smiles, thinking about how great it is to have a best friend who loves to cook.

He pulls out another pizza and declares, "This one is the Julie pizza!"

She laughs. "What exactly makes it the Julie pizza?"

"It's gluten-free, dairy-free, and has all of your favorite toppings. Made especially for you." He smiles. "Do you like that?"

"I love it!" She looks up at him, impressed, as he puts a few pieces on her plate.

He puts the pizzas back in the oven and they take their plates into the living room. Sitting on the sofa, they decide to dig into their dinners but wait for Allison to start the movie.

The sliding glass door shuts with a bang as Allison storms into the room. "Guess you couldn't wait?" she says with sarcasm.

"We just started eating . . . we were hungry, and Julie got here over a half hour ago, Allison," Nick says calmly. "The pizzas are still warm in the oven."

She gets her plate and comes into the living room, sitting in the armchair across from the sofa.

"It's good to see you, Allison," Julie greets her.

Allison ignores the pleasantry, her brows furrowing as she takes a bite of pizza. She looks over at Julie's plate and remarks, "I don't know how you eat that healthy pizza . . . it tastes like wet cardboard topped with dried celery."

Julie smiles and says, "It's delicious the way that Nick makes it." He smiles at her apologetically.

"Aren't you going to ask me about my call, Nick?" she asks coolly.

"I thought it would be better to talk about your business stuff later and to enjoy dinner and a movie now while Julie's here." He gets up to get another piece of pizza and returns with a piece of the special "Julie pizza" for himself and for Julie.

"Oh, thank you," Julie says as she graciously accepts it and refills their wine glasses.

Looking up from checking her phone, Allison asks, "Tell me how you two met again?"

Nick starts, "We were both attending a personal development conference and . . ."

"Oh, right, the cult!" Allison interrupts.

"It's not a cult, Allison," Nick says. "Some people actually like to work on themselves and become better human beings."

"Right," Allison says dismissively, and she goes back to checking emails on her phone. Nick looks at Julie. "Do you remember the day we met?"

Julie smiles. "Of course I do. You were in my group for one of the exercises and I was so impressed by your calm confidence, strength, and authenticity. I'd never met anyone quite like you before."

Nick says, "I remember that you were so heart-centered and gracious as you shared about your life. Your ambition and persistence really impressed me. And you were so humble."

"We had lunch that day and have encouraged each other as we've built our businesses over the past few years," says Julie.

He smiles. "Wow, you're right . . . that was before I bought my firm." He looks over at Allison. "And it was right after I started dating you." Nick smiles sweetly in her direction.

Allison glances up for a moment and asks, "Are we going to start the movie soon?"

Julie gathers everyone's plates and asks if anyone would like a refill. Both she and Nick head to the kitchen to clean up from dinner while Allison sits affixed to the armchair, wrapped up in her digital world.

When they finish washing the dishes and putting the pizza into the fridge, Julie says, "I think I might leave now, Nick."

"Why? We haven't started the movie yet, and it's one of your favorites."

Julie whispers, "I don't know . . . I'm not sure Allison likes me being here. It's just weird. She's being so negative, and I feel like it might be better for you if I just go."

He looks apologetic. "No, it's not personal . . . this is how she always is. It's just her dry personality." He takes her wine glass and sets it on the table. "Plus, you've had too much wine to drive yourself home for a while. I know you, and you're already drunk," he teases her.

She laughs. "You're very persuasive, Mr. Bliss."

Six

A few weeks later, Julie runs into Nick while working out at the gym. He sees her from across the room and goes over and gives her a big hug. "Hey Julie! It's great to see you."

"So good to see you, too! How are you?"

"I'm doing well. I haven't seen you for a little while. I was thinking about inviting you to a baseball game this week."

"I've been really focused on my writing and spending time with Evan. That would be fun, but I think Evan and I are going to do something this weekend."

Nick looks surprised. "Evan? Are you guys still seeing each other?"

"Yeah, we've had a few more dates since the last one I told you about."

"How's it going?" he asks with genuine curiosity.

"Honestly, I'm not sure. He's kinda unpredictable and runs hot and cold. Here's a picture we took together last weekend. He really wanted to take the picture but didn't want me to share it on Facebook."

Nick takes a look at the photo on her phone. "Handsome guy, but I don't like the sound of that. Are you happy with him?"

She thinks for a moment. "I'm not sure. He's a lot of fun, but I feel uneasy around him sometimes, too."

"Does he treat you well?"

"Most times," she says with hesitation, "but I think there's room for improvement. He doesn't like me spending time with you."

"Really? Is that why I haven't seen much of you lately?"

She nibbles her bottom lip. "I'm sorry . . . I feel awkward about it. I don't know why he's so insecure."

"Hmm." Nick shakes his head. "You have your big event on Saturday, right? Do you have plans for Thursday?"

"You have such a great memory . . . Yes, the event is all day on Saturday. As of right now, I'm free on Thursday night."

"Would you like to go to see the Dodgers play? I won two tickets at a business event. The game starts at 7:00 p.m., and it would be my treat." He smiles.

"Oh!" she says, thinking of how to respond. "That sounds like a lot of fun. Count me in!" She smiles as Nick gives her another squeeze.

"I've missed you over the past few weeks. We have to celebrate all the good stuff happening for you right now!"

"Thanks, Nick! Can't wait!"

"I had so much fun tonight, Nick!" Julie says as he pulls into the driveway of her apartment. "I still can't believe you caught that foul ball!"

He laughs. "I know, that was wild! Magic happens when I'm with you."

"I was really impressed that you gave it to that little kid."

"Well, I think it meant more to him that it did to me. He was all decked out in Dodgers gear, and the way his face lit up when I handed it to him was totally worth it." He smiles and gets out of the truck to open the door for her.

Walking her to the front door, Nick asks, "How are you feeling about Saturday?"

She takes off her Dodgers cap as they walk inside. "Excited . . . and a little nervous, as always. It's going to be a fun day."

"Is Evan going to be there?" he asks with hesitation.

Julie smiles. "He said he would come. I think that's why I feel nervous."

"You'll be great. Just be yourself. I'll be thinking of you. I know it'll be a successful day."

He gives her a hug and kisses her on the cheek. "Sleep well."

"Thanks again for the fun night out, Nick!"

He turns around, flashing a grin.

"Goodnight!"

Seven

After an exhilarating appearance on stage and being on her feet for eight hours at her largest book event yet, Julie is drained and ready to go home. Waiting on the loading dock for forty-five minutes without any sign of Evan, she doesn't know what to do, so she reaches out to Nick.

It feels like forever waiting for him to answer the phone.

"Hey Julie! I was just thinking about you. How'd it go today?"

Feeling grateful for the familiar warmth of his voice, Julie replies, "It went well, but I'm exhausted and can barely think right now."

"That's because you gave it your all. Proud of you!"

"So, Evan was supposed to be here . . . I haven't heard from him. I don't know what I'm going to do." She sits on her boxes with her head in her hands.

"What?! He isn't there?! That guy . . ."

Julie starts to cry. "I think I'm going to call a cab now. I don't know what to do with all of my boxes."

"Where are you?"

"I'm on the loading dock at the Staples Center . . ."

"I'll be there in thirty minutes. I'll bring my truck so we can carry your set-up. I'm leaving right now."

Choking back her tears, Julie replies, "Thank you, Nick."

A photographer walking by stumbles upon her sitting on her boxes and crying. He takes a few pictures of her from a distance and then approaches her from behind.

"Hi beautiful, I'm Will. Will Magnum."

Julie is startled and turns around to see an extremely handsome, tall, fit, and muscular man. She's so physically and emotionally exhausted that she can barely carry on a conversation. "I'm Julie."

"I know who you are," he says, and immediately launches into a monologue about himself. The words he's saying are completely boring her, but she distracts herself with his charming, million-dollar smile and finds herself nodding along, transfixed by his deep blue eyes.

Nick pulls up to the loading dock and sees Will talking with Julie. He feels relieved that she's not waiting alone now that the sun has started to set.

He gets out of his truck and approaches them, hands Julie a cold bottle of water and a piece of gluten-free pumpkin bread, her favorite.

"Hey Jules. Thought you could use some refreshment."

"Oh wow, thank you, Nick. You're the best!" she says as she throws her arms around him.

"Is this your assistant?" Will quips.

Julie looks incredulous. "No, this is my best friend, Nick." Nick sticks his hand out to shake and Will reluctantly does the same.

"Hi, I'm Nick . . . What's your name?"

"Will," and shoves a business card into his hand. Nick takes a glance at the card. "You're a photographer?"

Will pauses, casually glancing at the camera around his neck. "Uh, yeah."

"Nice meeting you." Nick starts loading Julie's boxes into his truck. Will continues talking to Julie while she picks up boxes and loads them alongside Nick.

When they're done loading, Will continues talking with Julie, undeterred. Nick comes over, puts his arm around her shoulders and says, "I'm going to get her home now. Take care, Will," and gently leads her to the truck.

"Give me your number, Julie," Will cuts in. "I'd like to photograph you sometime. I have some ideas that can take your business to the next level."

Julie reaches into her purse and pulls out a card for him. Turning back towards Nick's truck, she gives a small wave. "Bye, nice meeting you."

Nick walks her over to his truck, opens the passenger door for her, and closes it carefully once she's comfortably inside.

He gets into the driver's seat, and she sleepily smiles at him with a mouth full of pumpkin bread. "Thanks for picking me up, Nick."

He smiles devilishly. "Looks like I wasn't the only one trying to pick you up . . . Hey Julie," he says, turning towards her, "I have a weird feeling about that guy."

"Ummhmm," responds Julie while dozing off.

Nick pats her knee lightly, "It's okay. You rest." He pulls a sweatshirt from his back seat and props it under her head as a pillow. Eyes still closed, she smiles. The gentle whir of the truck engine lulls her fast asleep.

Julie wakes up as the dusk is setting in. The truck is still, and the driver's seat is empty. She looks around and is so tired she can barely keep her eyes open. Half-formed salt crystals are making her eyelids extra sticky and heavy. She obeys their wishes and rests her eyes again.

Nick opens the passenger door and gently rubs her arm. "Julie," he whispers, "you're home."

She can hardly open her eyes to look at him. "I'm so tired."

"Hold on." He vanishes and comes back a minute later. He tells her, "Put your arms around my neck," and scoops his strong arms under her legs and around her back. He easily lifts her out of the truck and carries her into her apartment. He lays her gently on the bed. "I'll be right back."

He leans close to her ear. "I unloaded all of your stuff. I know you're exhausted, so I'm going to leave and let you rest. I have a business dinner, so I've gotta run. Call me if you need anything." He slips her shoes off, pulls the covers up over her body, and locks the front door as he leaves.

Eight

As Nick gets into his truck, he sees a man coming around the corner walking toward Julie's gate. In the streetlight, he recognizes Evan from his picture. Nick gets out and approaches him before he can reach the handle.

"Hey buddy, where were you?" he says as calmly as he can muster.

"Oh, hey . . . you must be Nick," Evan replies sheepishly. "Something came up and I couldn't make it. No biggie."

"And you couldn't call?" Nick blurts out. The anger flashing in his eyes is partially concealed by the composure in his voice.

"It's really none of your business, Nick. I'm here to talk to Julie, not you," Evan snaps.

Nick stands steady, blocking the gate. "You left her stranded on the loading dock with all of her boxes after her biggest event ever without even calling to let her know you wouldn't be there . . ."

"I'm sorry to have inconvenienced you, Nick," Evan replies with sarcasm.

"You don't get it . . . helping Julie is never an inconvenience. I don't like to see her disappointed. It's not okay with me."

"Well, obviously you're her hero. Good for you, Nick," he says and tries to move past Nick.

"What are you doing?"

"I'm gonna go talk to her," Evan says as Nick moves completely in front of the gate.

"No . . . do you have any idea how exhausted she is? She had a huge day and then got stood up by her boyfriend—the one person she's supposed to be able to count on."

Evan looks down at the ground and mutters, "I'm not such a bad guy, Nick. It's complicated."

Nick looks Evan directly in his eyes. "I don't understand what's so complicated. There's an amazing woman in there whose big beautiful heart has been broken by a guy who clearly doesn't deserve her. Don't disturb her."

Evan pleads, "Come on, man. I feel bad enough. I thought she might be hungry . . . I brought her something." He pulls a Snickers bar out of his pocket, grinning smugly.

Nick sighs, shaking his head. "Julie is allergic to peanuts. You should know that already. She's so tired that she can't even keep her eyes open right now."

Evan chuckles a little. "Good, it'll be the perfect time to have this conversation," he says, and winks at Nick.

Nick's jaw tenses and he shakes his head. "I think you should leave, Evan. Let her rest, man."

"I really want to get this over with now."

"Goodbye, Evan," Nick says, standing like a statue in front of the gate.

Evan is shocked and begins slowly walking away. "You're not her boyfriend, Nick," he retorts from a distance.

"You're right. I'm her best friend, and I take that very seriously."

Nick stays resolutely in front of the gate until he sees Evan disappear. He checks his phone and lingers ten more minutes just to be sure that Evan doesn't come back before getting into his truck and driving to dinner. He likes to be on time, but it's worth being a few minutes late to protect Julie from that idiot.

Julie wakes up in a daze. She was so exhausted that she slept in her clothes. She gets up and looks in the mirror . . . hair jumbled up, dress twisted around her hips, and eyes smudged with makeup. *I keep meaning to get some waterproof mascara . . . seems like I need it these days.*

She frantically pats the messy bed looking for her phone . . . not there. Getting a bottle of water from the fridge, the light illuminates the counter and she sees it plugged into the charger. *Nick must've charged it for me. He thinks of everything. Thank God for Nick,* she thinks as she remembers what happened the day before.

She scrolls through her messages. One from her mom asking how the event went, three flirty and slightly scandalous messages from that photographer asking her out, one from Evan, and a "Good morning! How'd you sleep?" from Nick.

She eagerly opens the message from Evan, wondering what happened to him the day before and hoping he has a really valid, believable excuse. It's a long message . . . and not what she expects.

As Julie reads his text, her stomach turns in knots and her knees weaken. She drops to the floor and tears begin to dampen her cheeks.

Nine

Julie can hardly breathe between her sobs now.

What happened?

What did I do wrong?

What have I done to deserve this?

It's all she can do to hit 'forward' and send it to Nick.

Putting his shoes on for his Sunday morning gym session, Nick hears the happy tweet of his phone and reads Julie's text. *Oh no.* He's filled with anger and disgust.

He calls Julie . . . no answer. A moment later he tries again . . . no answer. He feels a tightness in his throat. Allison asks, "Everything okay?"

"No, Julie needs me. I'll be back this afternoon."

Allison rolls her eyes. "Seriously?" Distracted, he ignores her not-so-subtle protest and heads out the door.

Nick drives over to Julie's place in a blink. All the way there he keeps thinking about her and how she must be crushed. *Evan is such an idiot.*

He uses his key to open the gate and unlock her door. He knocks forcefully before opening it. One step in the door and he can hear Julie crying loudly.

"Julie . . . it's Nick. I'm here. Everything's going to be okay." He comes around the corner to find her in a heap upon the kitchen floor, still wearing yesterday's clothes. Her phone is on the counter out of her reach.

He rushes in and scoops her up in his loving arms. "Oh my God, Julie. I'm so sorry."

Julie just looks up at him, unable to speak. Nick strokes her hair, and she clings tightly to him. He gently picks her up and carries her to the bed. He grabs some tissues and brings them to her bedside.

She lies there on her stomach sprawled across the bed and sobs, throat burning, mascara running.

Nick softly strokes her back. "I have an idea . . . I know what will make you feel better." He looks deeply into her big, sad, green eyes and says, "I'm going to make you breakfast in the bathtub."

Julie looks at him through her tears and thinks he's sleep-deprived.

"This will be great," he insists. "Let's get you comfortable, and I'll make you something while you relax. I'll be right back." He disappears and she hears water running in her bathtub. Nick comes back carrying her fluffy bathrobe. "Okay, I've got the water and bubbles going." He lays her robe on the bed beside her. Julie almost wants to laugh at how over the top he's being.

"Get undressed and put this on. I'll wait outside your door." He leaves her bedroom, gently closing the door behind him.

Julie complies, still crying, but not as steadily now. She opens the door when she's in her robe. She's feeling so weak. Nick takes her in his arms and holds her tightly. Her feathery soft bathrobe feels soft against her skin in his tight embrace.

"You are so special, Julie. You deserve better than that fool." He kisses her forehead and leads her to the bathroom. Once she's inside, he closes the door. "Get comfy in there and I'll have breakfast ready shortly."

On the way to the kitchen, Nick pulls his phone out of his pocket and rereads her forwarded text.

> Hey Jules, I've been meaning
> 2 express this 2 u and think that
> now is the time 2 do so. I think u
> r an amazing woman that is a true
> gift 2 life. U r super sweet, thoughtful,
> and creative. Meanwhile, I feel horrible
> saying this, but I don't think we can
> continue 2 see each other. I am so
> busy with all these things I have going
> on in my life, and I'm not able to
> give myself fully 2 a relationship.
> I have been super down on
> myself cuz of the impact that it may
> have on u, but I don't want 2
> continue 2 lead u down a road that
> I won't b able 2 give. I hope 2 stay in
> ur heart in some way.

I hate that guy and the way he treats her. She's better off without him. He fumes about it while making banana pancakes for her.

A few minutes later he knocks on the bathroom door. "Come in," she calls to him. He slowly slips the plate through the cracked door, careful not to look in the direction of the bathtub.

"It's okay, Nick . . . I have the bubbles and the shower curtain."

He laughs and hands her breakfast plate and fork around the side of the shower curtain.

"Thank you, Nick. Please eat with me."

"Okay, I'll stay with you." He sits on the edge of the bathtub and eats his pancakes. "How are you feeling now?"

"So much better."

"I'm sorry that Evan is such a douche."

"I'm just so disappointed," she says with a mouthful of pancakes and tears rolling down her cheeks.

"I know. It's understandable," he assures her.

Julie peeks out from behind the shower curtain and smiles at him. "There's that smile! How are your pancakes?"

"Delicious! Banana pancakes are my favorite!"

"I know," he says quietly to himself and finishes his last bite.

She laughs a little and admits to him, "I've never eaten in the bathtub before."

He smiles. "Feels fun and a little scandalous, huh?"

"Totally." Her heart feels a momentary relief from the pain of rejection.

"So, what's the game plan for today, Julie? Can you take some time for yourself?"

"Today's a recovery day for me. No writing or events or media booked, thank goodness." She heaves a big sigh.

"I'm glad to hear that."

"Maybe I'll get some sleep," she says, finishing her food. "And what are you doing today?" she asks.

"I'm going to get you comfortable and then hit the gym. I'm having dinner with Allison tonight. It's a pretty low-key day. Are you turning into a prune yet?" he teases.

She sticks her hands out of the curtain. "Just about."

"Hand me your plate and I'll get you a towel."

Gathering their plates he says, "You know, I'm really proud of you, Julie. You are rockin' it, and you work so hard. No one has handed you anything in life. You earn it and deserve all good things."

"Thanks, Nick," she says as she towels off. "I'm just tired of being disappointed by guys. I don't understand it. A breakup via text??!!"

"I know. He's not playing the game of life on the same level as you. He's not even in the same sport. And it's better to know it now."

"Do you think I should respond to his message?"

"Not today. Maybe never. He can wait. Today is all about you."

She wraps the towel around her and emerges from behind the shower curtain into the bedroom. "Close your eyes, Nick." Nick complies. She drops her towel on the bedroom floor and climbs under the covers.

"You can open them now." He walks over and sits beside her on the bed. "I know you must be tired after the past day and night. I want you to call or text me anytime you need me."

She grabs his hand. "You've already done so much for me. I don't want to keep bothering you."

"Shhhh . . . You're my best friend. I love you, and I want to be here for you. You would do the same for me."

"That's true. I love you, too."

"Okay, get some rest. I'm gonna go, but I'll call you later to see how your day is going."

He ruffles her hair playfully and gets up to go. Julie calls out, "Nick." He turns around. "Thank you," she says, the familiar warmth returning to her voice.

Finally relaxed, Julie drifts off to sleep.

$\mathcal{T}en$

When she wakes up hours later, Julie rereads Evan's text message over and over and thinks there may be a misunderstanding. *I can't believe it's over. It felt like something was just beginning. We were just getting to know each other. I feel so rejected. It sucks being alone . . . and I've been alone for so long. Maybe he forgot about the event and was so afraid that I wouldn't forgive him that he broke it off instead?* She turns the possibilities over in her head, searching for the reasonable explanation that must exist. She decides to take a shower, put some makeup on, and go see him.

After carefully selecting her sexy lingerie and beautiful we're-back-together outfit and making sure her hair looks just right, she gets into her car to drive to his place.

On the way, she shores up her confidence by thinking about what she'll say to clarify the situation and resolve it quickly so they can kiss, make up, and move forward. She pictures him opening the door, looking surprised and relieved to see her.

She sees him in her mind's eye apologizing and tearing up at the damage he caused unintentionally. In her fantasy, he explains that he didn't communicate well and that he really wants her to forgive him, that he can't wait to be the man she always knew he was capable of being. She smiles at the relief she feels at the thought of it.

Pulling into his driveway behind his car, she hears the familiar crackle of the gravel beneath her tires and sees lights on in his windows. *Oh good, he's home.* Her heart swells with hope.

She gets out, bounces up the stairs on his front porch in her beautiful outfit, and knocks on the door eagerly but trying not to appear frantic. Her mind is full of images of the incredible make-out session they'll have after this misunderstanding gets cleared up. Maybe they'll even go further. She bristles with excitement, her pulse rushing as she imagines the door opening and his arms flying around her. She can't wait for him to realize his mistakes and choose her.

She looks in the peephole in a loving way so his first view of her will be to see how beautiful and understanding she is. She waits. No response, no movement inside, no romantic love scene unfolding like it did in her imagination. Nothing.

She stares at his closed door. Her heart starts to beat a little faster as she feels a hot bubble rising up into her throat from her chest. *This doesn't make any sense. Why won't Evan answer his door? Maybe he's asleep and can't hear me knocking?*

She takes a step back away from the door and hears the creaking of his porch beneath her. *What should I do?* She tries to hold back tears to avoid ruining her makeup. She sits down on his front step to collect her thoughts.

With anticipation, Julie decides to call him . . . no answer. It goes straight to voicemail, and she hangs up. Frustration and embarrassment wash over her. *What is going on here?*

Feeling hopeless, her efforts to hold back her tears fail. She had this grand plan to give him the opportunity to explain himself, to apologize, and to welcome him back with open arms. This is definitely not the way she pictured it. Unsure what to do next, she sits and waits.

She imagines that people in the neighborhood walking by must pity her. *I probably look like an idiot crying out here on the porch,* she thinks, which just makes her cry more while she feels sorry for herself.

Suddenly, the chirp of a text message breaks the silence. Her hope returns for a moment only to be crushed yet again when she reads a text from Evan: "I don't want 2 talk. Plz leave."

So he is home! Feeling desperate and humiliated, she tries to figure out how to respond.

She texts back, "I think we just have a misunderstanding, and I really want to talk about it together. It won't take long. I want to see you face-to-face." She pushes Send with a hopeful heart.

No response.

She sits and listens to the cars drive by as hot tears roll down her reddened face. *I guess it's really over.*

She lingers fifteen more agonizing minutes before finally deciding to leave. She texts a quick "never mind" and stifles her tears long enough to walk to her car with as much dignity as she can muster. *Stand tall and keep walking,* she tries to convince herself. *Don't let him see you cry anymore.* It's all she can do to keep it together while she starts the car and pulls out of his driveway. She gets away just before she breaks down in sobs. Again.

On her way home, she hears her ringtone. In an instant, she forgets everything. Her broken heart feels hopeful that it could be Evan calling her to apologize and ask for one more chance.

She glances at the screen and sees Nick's smiling face. "Hello?" she says as clearly as she can in the moment.

"Julie . . . it's Nick." She pauses a moment to catch her breath before responding.

Sensing something is amiss, he asks, "Are you crying? What's wrong?"

"Oh Nick. I did something stupid just now and I feel embarrassed," she gasps, holding back her tears the best she can.

"Do you want to talk about it? Wait . . . where are you?"

She sighs. "Driving home from Evan's place."

"Oh no. I'll meet you at your apartment."

Thinking about what happened, Julie feels so stupid for thinking she could fix things with a man who clearly doesn't care about her or her needs. She's disappointed in him and frustrated with herself.

Along the drive she thinks of how disinterested she was in him when they first met and how she didn't even want to go out with him. *Why did I let myself fall for him?* She berates herself on the way home.

She gets home two minutes before Nick arrives, pizza box in hand. "Hey Julie," he says lovingly, giving her a kiss on the cheek. "I thought you might be hungry so I picked up that vegan pizza you love. Pull up a slice and tell me what happened." He smiles his charming smile and sits down on her bed.

"That smells divine," she says as she sits next to him. Relieved to be crying in the privacy of her own home, she grabs a slice of pizza and tells Nick the story with all the sad and humiliating details.

He looks at her compassionately, listens, and holds her while she sobs. "I can't believe him. What an idiot!" he declares calmly, but firmly.

"*I'm* the idiot for ever getting involved with him. And then for believing that he was actually a decent person worthy of a second chance." She looks down at her pizza as a tear falls from her eye. "He knew I was there and didn't even answer the door."

"Look at me, Julie." She pulls her head up and looks directly into his big blue eyes. "You deserve a man who always opens the door . . . no matter what's going on with him."

Tears pour from her eyes and she hugs Nick tightly. "What would I do without you, Nick?"

He takes a deep breath and says, "You don't ever have to wonder about that."

Eleven

A few weeks later, the pain of the breakup has faded, and Julie has kept her promise to Nick not to correspond with Evan at all. It's difficult for her at first, because she so wants to believe he's a good man. But it is getting easier.

She keeps herself busy by hitting the gym, meditating, and volunteering at the local women's shelter. And at first, Julie's writing schedule is sporadic as she takes the time necessary to grieve over her lost relationship. But she realizes she feels best when she dedicates most of her time and energy to her novel.

She spends more time on her own, journaling and focusing on her business. She has fun outings with Jolene, takes long bubble baths, and plans special adventures for her friends. Things are going well even though she can still feel a hole in her heart left by Evan and his carelessness.

As time goes on, she gets stronger and gets back into her regular routine, working out at the gym in the morning and then going to her favorite beach café to eat lunch and write for a few hours on most days.

One day, after a challenging workout, she walks into her café and sits down in her bright and tight gym clothes. She gets the same thing every day, so the restaurant staffers just instinctively bring it to her, no need to place an order anymore.

She sees Bella, a friendly waitress at the café, come around the corner carrying her lunch. Julie is happy to see her and feels so hungry after her workout. She smiles and thanks her.

"Hi Bella, it's good to see you!"

Bella places her meal on the table in front of her. "It's good to see you, too. We've missed you over the past few weeks." Then she comes closer to her and leans over like she's straightening something on the table. Julie is surprised when Bella starts whispering to her.

"There's a guy who's been in here every day this week looking for you."

Julie flinches in surprise, but she continues to listen.

"A good-looking guy, about your height, and always carrying flowers. He asks about you and then waits for a while. When you don't come in, he throws the flowers away and leaves."

Julie raises her eyebrows, fully intrigued. "Has he ever given you his name?"

"No, just the same routine every day. Must be his lunch break or something. Just thought I should let you know that you have an admirer." She smiles as she walks away.

Julie takes a quick look around the restaurant. She delights in the possibility of a good-looking man bringing her flowers. At the same time, as she digests all this information Bella has given her, she cringes slightly as she wonders what this man's intentions are. *Is he some sort of stalker?*

She abandons the thought for now, puts her earphones in, and digs into her lunch. Words are flowing through her as she hand writes her novel into her special notebook.

It feels so wonderful to be writing again, something that she wasn't able to do for the past six weeks while she was healing her heart. She feels like she's in another world while she's writing, a world without time or boundaries. She luxuriates in the experience, losing track of time and her surroundings.

While she's writing, she doesn't notice that someone is walking up behind her. It's not until he sits on the bench next to her that she becomes aware of his existence and looks up with a shock. When she does, she gasps for a breath. Evan is there before her, sitting next to her, and looking terrible. He has a knack for showing up unannounced, it seems.

It takes a moment for her to take it all in. He looks the worst she's ever seen him.

He's wearing ill-fitting jeans, dirty tennis shoes, and what looks like a very old Rolling Stones t-shirt. His hair is a mess, his face full of stubble. His eyes are puffy, and he looks like he's gained at least fifteen pounds since she last saw him, all in his stomach and his face. *Whoa.* She remains speechless.

She's so stunned to see him, especially in his present condition, that she just sits there with her earphones in, still not saying a word.

Evan looks at her like a lost puppy dog that has found his way home. He glances down at the table and then back at her.

He pulls the earphones out of her ears. Startled by this gesture, she gently slaps his hands away from her.

"Julie, I'm so sorry about the breakup text message. I was wrong. I really miss you. I have intense feelings for you and allowed them to scare me. I thought my life was too busy for a relationship. But, after further thought, I'm clear that I want you in my life. I'm willing to do what it takes to create space for a relationship with you."

She sits there watching his mouth say the words that she so badly wanted to hear six weeks ago. She's dumbstruck.

He continues, "I'm sorry I hurt you. I've been thinking about you nonstop. I've never met anyone like you before. I can't imagine not getting to talk with you, see you, and be with you. I really want to be with you."

She says nothing. Nothing comes to mind to be said. Just an instant before he plopped himself onto the bench next to her and back into her life, she was feeling the freedom of inspiration and creativity flow through her as she poured her heart out onto the page. Now she's at a complete loss for the words that were coming so easily only moments before.

Sensing that what he's said so far is not enough to win her back, he adds, "I know you may be upset. I deserve that for being a loser and for hurting you. I hope that we can pick up from where we left off before I fucked it all up. I really care about you. I'm sorry." He hands her the flowers he had been holding in his lap.

Staring at him, she sits there and inhales. She doesn't reach out to accept the flowers. He sets them on the table in front of her, on top of her notebook.

Bella comes over to the table. "Just wanted to check on you, Julie. Is everything okay?"

Julie looks over at her and nods her head in slow motion, still unable to process the scene unfolding in front of her.

"Okay, just let me know if you need anything else," she says with a concerned smile as she clears Julie's lunch plate from the table.

Julie looks back at Evan.

Growing exasperated, he says, "Aren't you going to say anything?! I just poured my heart out to you and you're just sitting there like it doesn't matter."

She looks him in the eyes and can see some remorse, and also fear and anger. She calmly responds, "What do you want me to say, Evan?"

"Nothing," he says in a huff and turns his back to her.

She's familiar with his temper tantrums and decides not to give him the mothering attention that he's demanding.

Instead, she picks up her pen, slides the flowers off of her notebook, and pretends to go back to her writing.

Evan becomes indignant. "Are you just going to ignore me after I waited here for you for so many days?"

She replies without looking up from her notebook. "You mean like you ignored me when I was waiting for you after my event and then again when I was waiting outside your front door?"

He gets huffy and childishly says, "That was different. I just told you that I made a mistake. Aren't you going to forgive me?" he demands with desperation in his voice.

She looks up at him. "I don't think so, Evan. Not until I'm ready."

He gets up abruptly from the table, and it makes a loud screeching noise on the floor. The sound cuts into the friendly chatter of the café, and everyone turns to look at them. "Fine. Be that way. I don't forgive you either," he says sharply.

She calmly responds, "I haven't done anything to you, Evan."

He immediately shifts into a pleading mode. "Please just go out with me one more time and let me show you how much I've changed. I'm a better man now, I promise you."

"Really?" she asks almost sarcastically.

"Yes, let me show you." He smiles and a little of his charm comes through again despite his disheveled appearance and immature outburst.

All she can think about is making him go away so she can get back into the delicious flow of her writing again. "If I say yes, will you leave right now so I can finish my writing?"

The excitement drops from his face, but he quickly covers it up with a false smile and agrees.

"Okay, one more chance." She immediately feels regret that she's opening her heart to him again, even a little bit feels like too much. In spite of herself, she smiles inwardly at having had a man who rejected her begging in public for her to go out with him again.

"Yes!" he says while pumping his arm into the air like he just scored a goal in a soccer game. "I'll pick you up tomorrow at 8 then."

"See you then," she says. He leans down to give her a kiss on the lips. She turns her face so that he kisses her cheek instead. "Show me that you're a better man and then I may let you kiss me."

She can tell that he was hurt and angered by her implication that he hasn't changed. He always has such a grandiose view of himself. She feels proud of herself for not giving in to the volatile feelings she was experiencing in that moment and instead staying calm and handling the situation with confidence.

"Fine. I'll show you," he says and then leaves the café. At the doorway, he looks over at her and blows her a kiss and mouths "I love you." She just stares out the window for a moment after he walks away, then dives back into her work.

Twelve

After Evan leaves the café, Julie feels like she will burst if she doesn't tell someone what happened. She doesn't really know what to think about his behavior and wants to bounce some ideas off of one of her friends.

She dials Nick's number and then remembers that he's in an important meeting today. She cancels the call before she presses Send.

She texts Jolene, "You will never believe what just happened!"

Jolene calls her right away. "Hey chica! What's shaking?" she asks enthusiastically.

Julie tells her the whole story.

Jolene listens, riveted by the recent developments. "I told you that they always come back," she says with a smile. "How are you feeling about it?"

"Kinda confused. On the one hand, I'm happy that he realized that he fucked up with me and that he missed me. On the other hand, I don't feel like I can trust him, and that doesn't feel very good."

"That's understandable. I mean, he stood you up on one of the most important days of your career and then acted like a complete asshole when you tried to talk with him about it. I don't know about him."

"I still feel attracted to him and I've been doing well since we broke up, but I miss him," she admits.

"I know it feels that way. I'm not sure if you're missing him, or the idea of him. But, either way, you're doing the right thing by making him show you that he deserves your time and attention. Hey, I gotta run."

"You're so wise. Thanks for calling me. Love you!"

Jolene replies, "Can't wait to hear what Nick thinks of all this. Love you, too!"

Me too, Julie thinks.

When she hangs up the phone, Bella comes over to the table. "How are you doing?"

"Fine," she says as she picks up the flowers and sniffs them. "I love roses."

"That was the guy I was telling you about," Bella says. Julie smiles slightly and nods.

"But I have to tell you that he's not a good man for you," she confides as she wipes the table.

Julie is shocked at Bella's forwardness. "What do you mean?"

"I don't know . . . there's just something about him. You radiate joy and sunshine, and he seems like more of a wet blanket who wants all the attention for himself. Everyone loves you here. I'm just looking out for you," she shares apologetically as she comfortingly cups Julie's hand.

"Thanks, Bella. I appreciate the courage it took to share that with me." *She's probably right. Evan isn't exactly my dream guy. But, I'm glad he realized his mistake and wants me back. Sometimes I feel so confused. I'll just see how it goes for now.*

Facing the reluctant truth that her creative spark has dimmed for the day, she packs up her notebook, pens, and flowers and heads home.

After a warm shower, Julie is happy and refreshed again. She accomplished her workout, made great progress on her novel, and got the apology that she daydreamed about from Evan. She can't wait to tell Nick about it.

She texts him, "Hey Nick! Can't wait to hear about your meeting. You'll never believe what happened today. How about dinner at my place?"

He texts back a few minutes later, "Hi! Great meeting. 7 p.m.? Want me to bring Indian?"

She smiles. He knows her so well. "Perfection," she answers.

When Nick arrives, he's wearing his best business suit and looking incredibly dapper, a stark difference from the way that Evan appeared earlier that day. "Wow! You look gorgeous, Nick."

He smiles. "Thank you! I hope you're hungry. I couldn't decide between the fish and the saag so I got both . . . and lots of garlic naan." He pulls a bottle of champagne from the bag. "And, some sparkles to celebrate."

Julie wraps her arms around him and gives him a big squeeze. "Do you have any idea how awesome you are?" They both laugh.

She gets out the plates and the champagne flutes as he removes his suit jacket and prepares their feast.

"Tell me about your day, Julie."

"You tell me first."

They carry their plates to the bed and lean up against her headboard. With pillows supporting their backs and propping the plates on their laps, they dig in.

Nick holds up his glass. "Cheers to us both having productive days," he says, "and to getting to celebrate together." He clinks his glass to hers, and they both take a sip.

"So, the meeting today was a big success. Our firm won our biggest contract yet, and I'm excited to design a brand new building in downtown LA. They loved our designs, and it's going to be more lucrative than we originally projected." He smiles.

"That's so wonderful! Wow. Congratulations, Nick! You deserve it," she says and clinks glasses again. "Cheers."

"How's Allison doing?" Julie asks.

"She's fine. She's on a business trip in Seattle again this week. It's perfect for her because she loves the rain." He smiles. "Now tell me what happened today. You were so mysterious. I'm intrigued."

She smiles and shifts in her seat. Earlier, she was excited to tell him about Evan. Now she's feeling like it doesn't really matter. She decides to share anyway.

Julie tells him the full story about Evan coming to her café and waiting for her every day for a week, how he had flowers for her, and the things that he said. She recounts the conversation as best she can and takes a deep breath. "So, what do you think?"

Nick contemplates everything she shared for a moment and then asks, "Do you want my honest, unfiltered opinion?"

She feels a little nervous but says yes.

He sets his fork down on the side of his plate and says, "Evan is a douche. Of course he misses you—you're amazing, and when you're around, he receives constant attention, affection, and validation. Evan is a little boy who wants someone to mother him. My guess is he was seeing someone else when you knocked on his door that day, and rather than be honest about it, he weaseled his way out of your relationship via text message. Now that person is probably long gone and he sees what he's missing, so he's coming back to manipulate you again."

She listens intently.

"I'm sorry to say it, Julie, but I don't like the way he stalked you, presumptively sat with you, yanked your ear buds out, and demanded that you accept his apology and go out with him again. Those aren't things that a respectful person would do. You have my full support whatever you decide, but this guy is just wasting your time."

He hands her a piece of naan and refills the saag on her plate. "Thank you," she says, "for being so open with me. I see what you're saying."

"You've been doing so well over the past few weeks. You don't need him or his drama bringing you down. Stop settling for mediocrity."

Julie feels her face flush with heat as Nick says that last sentence. One thing she never wants to be is mediocre. "I'm not mediocre, Nick."

"No, of course you're not. It's just that you are putting yourself into unhealthy situations with a disrespectful man. You're creating your own drama."

A combination of shame, fear, and embarrassment overcome her and shut down her internal filters. "I'm doing the best I can right now. I'm so tired of being alone," she responds defensively.

"I know you are. But being alone is better than being with the wrong person. I'm not trying to hurt your feelings, Julie. I just want you to see that you're on the path to mediocrity with this man."

Feeling heated now, she says matter-of-factly, "It's not like you're super happy in your life either, Nick. You're settling for mediocrity, too, you know." She regrets saying it immediately after the words spew from her mouth.

Nick's jaw tightens as he looks down at his plate and contemplates her words. They sting. He sits in silence and slowly his eyes return to meet hers.

Oh my God. I hurt him. Look at his eyes. Why did I say that?

He stares at her for a moment and then softens his jaw. "You could be right. There are aspects of my life in which I've grown comfortable, and maybe I'm not as happy as I could be." He drinks from his champagne glass. "Julie, I only want to help you."

"I'm sorry, Nick. That was a jerky thing for me to say—I shouldn't have said it. You are so wonderful to me, and I know you're only trying to help." She leans over and gives him a hug.

He hugs her in return. In his mind he's wondering what areas of his life he's settling in, and it bothers him that she could be right.

"I know it sounds silly, but what if Evan really has changed?" she asks vulnerably.

Nick looks at her with compassion but says, "I assure you that he hasn't changed."

"How do you know?"

"Because I've been around guys like that my whole life. He will always be a little boy who acts like a dog. Guys don't really change who they are at their core. Even if he wanted to, it would be a completely uphill battle, and he's not man enough for the journey."

"Will you judge me if I go on that one last date with him?"

He sighs. "I wish you would see that your time is too precious to waste on guys like that. But, no, I won't judge you. I love you unconditionally." He leans over and kisses her forehead.

Thirteen

The next night, Julie is buzzing with excitement to get to go on one more date with Evan. *Who knows, maybe he really has changed?* She puts on her prettiest, most form-fitting dress, curls her hair, and sprays her favorite perfume.

It's been six weeks since she's been on a date, and she loves the idea of making him suffer throughout the night. Walking past her vanity mirror, she takes a glance at herself. *I actually look pretty. I love how this gold jewelry sparkles and shines. Much better than the sweats I've been wearing lately.*

As she's grabbing her glittery gold purse, she checks her phone to see what time it is: 7:45 p.m. There's a voicemail waiting. *That's funny . . . I didn't even hear the phone ring.*

She turns her phone on speaker while she applies a deep red lipstick. She hears Evan's voice,

"Hey Jules. Listen, something's come up and I'm not going to be able to make it tonight. Talk to you later."

Her heart plummets deep into her stomach with a thud. *How could he do this to me again?!* She feels outraged and embarrassed and hopeful and ridiculous all at the same time.

She calls him up and is surprised when he actually answers the phone.

"Hey," he says shortly.

"I got your voicemail," she says, trying to hold back her anger.

"Yeah, sorry about that . . . " his voice trails off.

"I was looking forward to seeing you tonight."

"Me too. I've just got so much to do."

His excuse annoys her. "To do?"

"Yeah, my laundry has really piled up, and by the time I get it done, it'll be too late to have dinner."

"Evan, I'm telling you I want to see you, and you're telling me you'd rather do laundry," Julie says exasperatedly into the phone. "You're crazy."

"It's not that I'd rather do laundry. It's just that I have to get it done. It's not that I don't want to see you."

She feels a burning sensation in her throat and a pain in her gut. *This guy is never going to grow up and be a man.* "Got it. Have a good life, Evan," she says, and hangs up.

Why did I ever give him a chance to make anything up to me? Nick was right. He's a douche, and he's never going to change.

Her phone rings. She sees Nick's smiling face show up on her phone and answers it.

"Hey Julie! I know you're getting ready to go out, but I just wanted to run something by you real quick . . ."

"Hi Nick, I'm not going out tonight, so take your time." She tries not to sound too disappointed even though she just spent an hour getting ready for a date that's not going to happen.

"What do you mean? I thought Evan was going to explain himself and attempt to show you that he's a new man tonight."

"Me too. Apparently doing his laundry is more important than spending time with me."

"*Laundry?* What's wrong with this guy? He's the only man on the planet who would choose laundry over going out with you. He's so lame."

"I know . . . I finally see it. You were right. It's disappointing. I'm tired of his bullshit, and I'm ready to be done with him."

"I'm sorry he sucks, but I'm happy to hear your vow to move forward. He's an anchor, and you don't need that holding you back."

"Thanks, Nick. Too bad I'm all dressed up with no place to go," Julie says with the glimmer of a smile in her voice. "What did you want to talk to me about?"

"Oh . . . it's about your birthday."

"I almost forgot," she says, laughing.

"Don't worry, it's going to be awesome. Do you trust me?"

"You know I do."

"Good, then I'll make it a surprise!"

"Sometimes you make me nervous, Nick."

Nick laughs. "Don't worry . . . you'll love it!"

"About tonight," he continues. "I haven't eaten yet, and I'm just leaving the office. Do you want me to swing by and take you out?"

Julie's heart leaps. "Oh, that would be amazing, Nick!"

"See you in twenty minutes!"

"Can't wait!" she says and hangs up.

While waiting for Nick to arrive, Julie looks in the mirror and stares into her own eyes. She knows she did the right thing by saying goodbye to Evan. *He's obviously not serious about his own life, much less about me.*

Sometimes I wonder if love is really worth it. Maybe my life would be simpler without thinking about love and its complications.

She hears Nick's familiar knock on the door. She goes to open it and his eyes boggle out of his head when he sees her. "Oh my God, Julie! You look incredible! Wow. That turquoise dress is great on you." He gives her a hug.

"Thank you, you definitely brightened my evening with your call," she says while grabbing her purse and a wrap.

He offers his arm to her. "Are you ready?"

She takes his arm and squeezes his bicep. "Ready!"

"Lucky me, taking such a beautiful woman out to dinner tonight," he says as he opens the passenger door of his truck for her.

As she's getting into the truck, she sees Evan, of all people, walking toward them on the sidewalk. He's disheveled and looks angry. "Oh no," she says and looks up at Nick.

Nick looks over his shoulder and assures her, "Don't worry. I'll make him go away." He quietly closes her door and calmly stands ready to face Evan when he reaches them.

"So this is how it is!" Evan exclaims. "You can't take my girl out, Nick!"

Julie stares down at the ground. She doesn't like seeing Evan in this condition. He is drunk, out of control. She never realized before what an angry man he is. She also feels embarrassed that she was actually looking forward to going out with him and allowed him to reject her . . . again.

Nick motions for her to stay in the truck. "Evan, look man, she's not your girl. You don't own her. You let her down, and there's nothing more to say about it."

Evan looks desperately at Julie through the window and tries to talk to her. "You didn't give me another chance. You said you'd go out with me tonight," he reminds her.

Smelling the alcohol on his breath, Nick guides Evan away from the truck and says, "You were the one who canceled plans on her, remember? She doesn't owe you anything."

Evan takes a halfhearted swing at Nick and misses. Nick doesn't flinch, just stands there, unmoving.

Evan whines, "I just wanna talk to her for a minute."

"Sorry, man, but we've gotta go, and so do you," Nick says firmly.

Dumbfounded, Evan just stands there on the sidewalk as Nick gets into the truck, shuts the door, and drives away.

As they're heading around the corner, Julie looks back at him, and Evan raises his hand in a little sad wave.

Once they get a few blocks away and out of sight, Nick pulls over on the side of the road. He calls a cab and gives them Julie's address for pick up. He looks over at her. "Sorry, he's been drinking and I just want to make sure that he gets home alright without hurting himself or anyone else."

Julie marvels at him. *What an incredible man to not only save the day for me, but for Evan, too.*

"Now our evening can officially begin," he says cheerfully.

"That was kinda crazy, huh?" Julie says.

"Yeah, it was a little atypical," he replies with a smile.

"I honestly don't know what I ever saw in him," she says with shame.

"You saw what he wanted you to see. It's okay, you see the real him now." He pats her knee. "I was thinking maybe we'd get some sushi tonight. How does that feel to you?"

She perks up. Sushi is one of her favorites. "That sounds fun and delicious!"

He parks and walks around the truck to open her door for her. She takes his hand. "You're such a gentleman. I'm not used to this treatment."

"This is how you deserve to be treated, Julie," he says as he holds the restaurant door open for her.

Outside, the sign says "Sushi-Yo" in bright green neon letters. Inside it looks like a sushi bar frozen in time from the

'80s. They're playing *Ghostbusters* on a neon jukebox. Old-fashioned pinball machines light up the corner. The booths are themed after popular bands and movies.

"Wow! I love this place already!" she says as her eyes explore the colorful scenery.

"I had a feeling you might like it," Nick says as he guides her to a booth that is decked out with *Back to the Future* movie memorabilia.

She's having so much fun looking at the treasures on the walls that she forgets to look at the menu.

The waiter stops by to take their order. "I'm so hungry, but I haven't picked something yet," she apologizes.

"No problem," says Nick. "Why don't we share the sushi love boat?"

"Ooh! I've always wanted to get sushi on one of those pirate ships!"

"It has great sushi on it that I know you're gonna love." He enjoys watching her bubble with excitement.

When the sushi love boat arrives, she playfully claps her hands and cheers. She and Nick laugh out loud. "I wanna take a picture of you, Julie!" says Nick.

"Sure." She smiles and pretends to hold the sushi boat.

The waiter returns to the table and offers to take a picture of them together. "Absolutely," says Nick, and he switches over to her side of the booth. They pose together with the sushi boat and then he kisses her on the cheek before moving back to his side.

"You are so much fun, Julie!" he says as he grabs a few pieces of sushi and puts them on his plate.

"I always have fun with you!" she says, sampling a piece of delicious tuna.

He shows her the picture of them on his phone. "Wow! What a great photo."

"Is it okay if I post it later?" he asks.

"Yes." She settles into her seat, gazing at the colorful array of sushi and kind man in front of her. She's even happier that he wants to share their pictures publicly, something that Evan never wanted to do.

"How was your day, Nick?" she asks while enjoying a piece of eel.

He smiles. "It was very full and productive. Making progress on our biggest projects and got the city's approval on one of our more modern design proposals. Things are going well."

"You're such a rock star! Can't wait to see your newest design!"

"Really?" he asks honestly.

"Really. You do amazing work," she says while sipping her water.

"Would you like to come down and take a tour of my office next week? I'd love to show you some of our projects, introduce you to the team, and take you out to lunch at my favorite spot."

Between bites, she responds, "That sounds awesome. Let's set it up."

"Okay," he says in disbelief.

"Why is it so surprising that I'd want to see where you work and what you're working on?"

He thinks for a moment while getting a hold on his chopsticks. "It's just that Allison goes into sleep mode whenever I talk about my firm or my ideas for new projects. We've dated for three years now, and she still hasn't been to my office. I've invited her, but she always has something more pressing to do." He runs his hand through his hair and shrugs.

"Hmm . . . well, I guess with tax season and everything, it's busy for her," she says politely.

"You're running a much more successful business than she is, and she acts as if it's always tax season. But that doesn't matter right now. What matters is that we're here, having fun, and enjoying a sushi feast . . . in a boat!" They both laugh.

The waiter comes by to check on them and offers them each a complimentary cup of their finest sake as a gift from the owner. He sets the cups down on the table.

"Have you ever had sake, Julie?" he asks, picking up his cup.

She picks up the cup and gives it a sniff before pulling back and making a face. "No, should I?"

"If you're curious." He smiles and takes a sip.

She looks at the mysterious milky white liquid and swishes it around in the cup. She raises it up to her lips and looks at Nick with a mischievous smile. "Bottoms up," she says and takes a sip.

"You are so adventurous," Nick says with delight. "What do you think?"

"It's not too bad, not too good, and very strong." She sticks her tongue out for emphasis. "It burns my lips."

He laughs. "Do you want something else to drink?"

"No, that's okay. I think I'd rather save it for some after-dinner ice cream." She winks at him and hands him her almost-full sake cup.

He gratefully accepts her gift and raises it up as if to toast her before taking a sip. "Ice cream it is."

"I almost forgot to tell you . . . I wrote over 10,000 words in my novel today."

"Wow, that's awesome! It'll be so great to read it," he says while finishing his sake.

"When the Going Gets Tough, the Tough Get Going" starts playing on the jukebox.

"Oh, I love this song! Billy Ocean rocks! I haven't heard it in so long," she says and starts singing along to the lyrics and dancing in her seat.

"You make me smile," he says and starts singing along with her.

They sing and laugh together. The waiter comes over to wrap up their leftovers, and Nick asks him to turn up the music.

"You're so awesome," she says as they continue their duet.

When the song ends, she looks over at Nick as if seeing him for the first time. "I've never heard you sing before." She laughs. "As a matter of fact, I've never sung with anyone before."

He thinks for a moment. "I don't think I've ever sung in front of anyone before. You bring something different out in me." He gives her a big smile and goes up to the register to pay for their dinner.

When he gets back to the booth, he offers her his hand and then twirls her once just for fun. "I love being with you, Julie," he says in a confessional tone. "Now let's go get you some ice cream."

"That was the best sushi dinner I've ever had," she announces as he opens the restaurant door for her.

He smiles and says, "I really enjoyed it, too." He looks up into the night sky. "What a beautiful night."

"Hey I have a crazy question for you," she says as he walks alongside her carrying their doggy bag.

"Does it have to do with ice cream?" he asks playfully.

She gets a devilish look in her eyes. "Hmm . . . not exactly."

"I'm going to be bold and just say yes." They both laugh.

"Okay, let's get ice cream first, and then . . . a surprise!" She's elated that Nick is up for her ideas in a way that no man she's ever dated has been.

"What have I gotten myself into?" he asks, laughing, and puts his arm around her.

She kisses him on the cheek. "I like that I can just be myself with you."

"You are the whole package, Julie. You're a breathtaking beauty who's smart, successful, and fun. You've got it all."

"Is this the ice cream place?" she asks, looking at a store they're about to pass.

"Oh, yes, this is the spot. I was so deep in our conversation that I almost missed it," he laughs.

Inside they marvel at all the flavors. Julie asks to sample six different types with the mini shovels they give her. "There are so many. It's hard to decide. I want to taste them all." She laughs. "What are you getting?"

"I'll have mint chocolate chip."

"Yum!" After her taste test, she decides on "Rainbow Sprinkle Birthday Cake" along with plain vanilla in a waffle cone.

They decide to sit outside and enjoy the warm weather while they indulge in dessert.

"I can't remember the last time I had ice cream. How about you?" he asks.

"Gosh, it's been so long. Do you want to taste mine? The rainbow cake is scrumptious." They both laugh. She extends her cone over to his mouth. He looks curious and then takes a lick.

"Wow! That's some good stuff. Thank you."

She giggles. "You barely tasted it. Here, have a real taste." Julie pushes her ice cream cone into his lips leaving an ice cream ring around his mouth. They both chuckle as he wipes it off.

He takes a spoonful from his bowl and offers it to her.

She opens her mouth playfully and he feeds it to her. "I like that. And the ice cream is good, too." She laughs.

"I have fun with you, Julie."

"I'm glad you feel that way because you're in for even more fun tonight."

After they finish their ice creams, they walk along the sidewalk and she leads the way down the street and around the corner. She grabs his hand and walks into a divey-looking bar. "Uh, where are you going?" He tugs at her hand in the doorway.

She turns around and smiles at him. "You'll see. Come on."

They walk in and go past a nearly empty bar with dusty looking tables and big, bearded patrons. Nick is unsure what she's up to, but he trusts her.

She walks confidently through a beaded curtain into a smoky backroom, still holding his hand. When they get into the darkened room, he sees a disco ball, swirling lights, a stage, and a microphone.

"What is this?"

"Karaoke," she says happily.

They sit in one of the booths in the back and watch people go up and sing their songs. Nick looks around nervously. "I don't know if I can go up on stage and sing."

"Of course you can, you can do anything," she says.

"I did say yes, didn't I?"

"Yes, you did. And it's okay, I've never done it before either. I always just come by myself and watch other people having fun. We can do it together. I know the perfect song."

"Oh my God," he says and starts sweating and drying his hands on his pants legs.

"Do you trust me? Come on," she says and mischievously grabs his hand.

He follows her on stage. She turns to him and whispers, "No one knows us here, let's just have fun with it. Go full out, like the unstoppable Nick I know."

She hands her phone to a burly man in the front row to record them.

Nick reluctantly picks up the microphone as if an alien has taken over his body. She smiles at him widely.

His adrenaline is pumping, and he can barely feel his legs. They're standing on stage and the spotlight is so bright that he can't see anyone in the room but Julie. The music comes on, and he's happy to recognize the tune.

They both start singing timidly and gradually grow louder.

Nick and Julie look at each other and sing their hearts out, instantly forgetting that there's even an audience watching.

At the end of the song, they're both having so much fun singing that they almost forget they're on stage. The invisible crowd goes wild, cheering and clapping for them more than they did for any other performer.

Julie gets her phone back from the burly guy in the front row and thanks him for recording their duet. He says to Nick, "You and your girlfriend did a great job. Song of the night!"

"Oh thank you, but she's not my girlfriend," says Nick very respectfully.

"Well, she should be!" he says.

He grabs her hand and follows her outside. "I gotta tell you, Julie, I was really anxious when you walked into that place. I had no idea that you liked to watch karaoke."

"Yeah, it's not something I share with other people because I've never had the courage to actually go up on stage and do it myself . . . until tonight. So thanks for helping me overcome my fear." She smiles.

"Thank you for bringing me here . . . and on stage. That was such a great time . . . a big rush for me. Who knew?" He hugs her from the side.

"I had a feeling that we would both enjoy it. I know I can be a little eccentric at times—some people can't handle it," she laughs. "Thanks for indulging me. You're a brave man."

"This was perfect. I had a great time . . . sushi, ice cream, karaoke . . . and all on a weeknight. Let's get you home."

When they get back to her place, Nick parks his truck and walks her in. "How are you feeling now?"

"I'm on cloud nine, thanks to you and our magical night. I honestly had so much more fun with you than I've ever had with Evan, or with anyone now that I'm thinking about it." She laughs. "Thank you."

"Thank *you,* Julie," he grins. "See you soon."

After he leaves, she reflects on the day and how, even though it didn't go exactly the way she anticipated, it ended up being better than anything she could have hoped for. She gets ready for bed and lies down. She remembers the video from the karaoke bar and gets excited to watch it.

"Oh my God, it's so good," she says out loud. She texts the video to Nick with a note: "Sweet dreams, Rock Star! ☺"

She falls asleep with a smile on her face and a song in her heart.

ℱourteen

"I'm so confused," Julie says to Jolene.

Jolene looks at her for a moment and says, "What's confusing? He's not being a man. You want to know what a man is? Think about how Nick tells you how amazing you are, how you deserve the best, and how much he can't wait to see you next all the time. Evan is just wasting your time."

Jolene continues, "You shared something really special with him, Julie. And he acts so blasé about it. You deserve a man who pines for you and communicates with you daily."

Julie thinks about what Jolene has said. "You know what? You're right. Thank you for your honesty and for the clarity."

She gets a text on her phone and finds a message from Nick along with the pictures from the sushi restaurant: "Had a fun night with you. Hope you're feeling better. Talk with you soon. Long live the Karaoke Queen!"

She smiles and shows the text and photos to Jolene.

"Sweet! You need a normal guy like Nick," she declares.

Julie smiles and says thoughtfully, "Nick is definitely not normal. That's one of my favorite things about him."

They both laugh in agreement.

"Well it's been great catching up, Jolene. I gotta get started on my writing for today," says Julie.

"It has. I always enjoy our chats." They hug. "Love you, chica!"

"Love you, too," she replies as Jolene leaves the café.

Julie stares down at the table, studying the wood grain. She has clarity now about Evan and feels stronger than ever about waiting for someone special. She's surprised to realize that she hasn't even felt compelled to text him since everything went down the night before.

Thank God for Nick. He turned last night's pity party into a real party. She smiles remembering his face when she pulled him on stage and how trusting and brave he was to follow her lead. *Evan never would've done that with me.*

She pulls out her notebook and begins to write again.

A few days later Julie calls Nick. "Oh my God, Nick!" Something crazy has happened, and I have to share it with you!"

"What is it?" he asks excitedly.

"There's a lot of background noise. I can barely hear you. Is this a bad time?" she asks.

"No, no. I'm in a busy restaurant at a business meeting, but you're important to me and I want to hear your news. Hold on a second."

He walks outside of the building and says, "Okay, is this better?"

"Much better! I just received a call from the publishing company I told you about and they made me an incredible offer to publish my books!"

"That's amazing!" says Nick excitedly.

"You're not going to believe this . . . they offered me a $2 million-dollar advance, Nick!"

"Wow! I'm so happy for you. I knew it. No one deserves it more than you. We have to celebrate," he insists.

"Can't wait!" Julie agrees.

"Where are you writing today? I can leave the office early and take to you dinner tonight."

"That would be fun. I'm at my usual café. See you at five?"

"Sounds good. Big congrats, Julie, this is great news."

Nick arrives at the café on time with a beautiful mini bouquet of rainbow roses. He hugs her while picking her up and spinning her around.

Bella stops by and asks, "Hey Julie, who's this?"

Julie laughs. "Oh, Nick, I'd like you to meet my friend, Bella. She takes excellent care of me here at the café when I'm writing."

"Nice to meet you, Bella," he says while shaking her hand.

"Very nice to meet you, too." She gives Julie a conspiratorial smile. "Can I get you two anything?"

"No thank you, we're heading out for the night. See you tomorrow."

Nick takes a look at her and smiles. "It's so great to see you. I can't wait to hear all about your publishing deal."

Julie grins. "Thank you, Nick. I'm excited to celebrate!"

"Julie, you're glowing. You look amazing, and I'm taking you to a special place tonight. I hope you love it!"

He drives to Maestro's along the ocean, a very upscale place with gorgeous views, delicious food, live music, and excellent service.

As they walk into the restaurant and get seated with a breathtaking sunset view of the ocean, Julie says, "You're the best, Nick. Sometimes I get down because I don't have a boyfriend to celebrate moments like this with me. But, there's no one I'd rather spend this night with but you."

Nick smiles and looks deeply into her eyes. "So, now that you have the big deal and are awash in abundance like we always knew you would be, what's next?"

"Well . . . I think I'll buy that oceanfront estate I've been dreaming of—in cash, and then put the rest into my savings and investments for travel, expenses, and growing my business. I'm also going to give some money to local charities and help my family out a bit."

"That's a great plan," says Nick. "I would love to help you go house shopping. It'll be fun to help Barbie pick out her dream house," he says with a playful smile.

Julie enjoys the way his eyes light up and sparkle when he looks at her and how he gets excited about things. "Absolutely, let's do it!"

Fifteen

The following week, Julie tours Nick's office, meets his staff, and goes out to lunch with him.

"Hey," she says. "Remember the photographer we met at the Staples Center?"

Nick looks up in the air, scrunching up his face as if he's thinking for a moment. "The lazy guy with all the muscles?"

Julie giggles. "Yes, that's the one. He texted me again last night."

"What did he say?" he asks, taking a bite of his sandwich.

"He asked me out."

Nick swallows and says, "That doesn't surprise me. Are you gonna go out with him?"

"Well, it's just a coffee date. No big deal."

Nick frowns. "I don't like that, Julie. A coffee date is a lame way for him to be able to exit quickly in case he loses interest fifteen minutes after you get there. You deserve a proper date . . . like dinner and a movie. Plus, you don't even drink coffee."

"I love how you're so protective of me, Nick."

"I want you to have fun. Just watch out for that guy, okay?"

"Alright."

Julie arrives at her favorite café early to meet Will for their coffee date. She figures she might as well do some writing before he gets there. Out of the corner of her eye, she sees Bella walk into the café. "Hey Bella!"

"Hi beautiful! How's your writing going today?" She smiles.

"Just getting started. I'm meeting someone here for coffee."

"Oh, the friend who was in here yesterday?" she asks suggestively.

Julie laughs. "No, not Nick. A different someone."

"Now that guy is the right guy for you."

Julie laughs again and runs her hand through her hair. "What makes you think that?"

"I just have a feeling about him," she says matter-of-factly and walks away.

Julie thinks for a moment and smiles. For now, she's focusing on her novel. Those words aren't going to write themselves. She only has forty-five minutes to write until Will gets there.

She's so engrossed in writing her newest love scene that she doesn't even notice that it's twenty minutes past the time their date was supposed to begin, and Will hasn't arrived yet.

Bella comes over to say goodbye now that her shift has ended. Julie awakens from her trance and looks at the time. *Wow . . . he's late, very late.* She packs up her laptop to leave.

As she gets ready to walk out the door, she's surprised to see Will standing outside talking to another woman. She stops and hides behind the curtain so she can get a feel for what's going on. They seem friendly, like maybe they already know each other. He's smiling and talking a lot . . . as usual.

The woman is very beautiful and probably five to ten years younger than him. *Maybe she's his sister?* Then she sees him give her his card. It looks like she's giving him her number as he types something into his phone. *Okay, so probably not his sister.*

Julie feels ill. Obviously this guy fancies himself as a player, just like Nick said. She goes to the ladies' room to collect herself before leaving. While she's washing her hands, the woman he was talking to on the sidewalk comes into the restroom.

She tries to act cool and then notices that the woman drops Will's card as she's walking to the sink.

"Oh, you dropped something," she says as she points at the card on the floor.

The woman smiles and says, "I don't need it." She seems so confident.

Julie tries not to stare but then can't help but ask her, "How do you know?"

The woman smiles again and says, "I just do."

She leaves the restroom, ready to go home and get some dinner started now that her evening is a bust. She can't help but admire the woman's cool confidence about not wanting to get in touch with Will. She wishes that she felt that same way, but Julie rarely feels easy breezy about anything in her life.

As she gets ready to walk out the front door, Will grabs her shoulder and stops her. "Hey stranger!" He attempts to give her a hug.

"Hi, Will. I was just leaving," says Julie, shrinking away.

"Leaving? Why? You just got here."

"Actually, I've been here for hours writing, and you are super late, so I'm super uninterested in continuing this conversation."

He looks shocked yet satisfied, as if he's having the time of his life playing a game. "Don't leave. My shoot ran late this afternoon . . . it's all part of the life of Will Magnum. Let's just sit and chat for a few minutes."

Will's persistence both annoys and slightly intrigues her. She looks around and decides to sit for a few minutes.

"Great! I'll get you a coffee," he says, walking up to the counter.

"No thank you," she calls after him. "I'm good with just water."

He shrugs. "Suit yourself," he mutters, and continues to the counter with his order.

Julie's gut is telling her to leave now and salvage her evening with a nice glass of wine in the bathtub. But she feels bad going after she agreed to stay for a short chat. She promises herself she'll only stay for fifteen minutes. *Why do I get myself into these situations?*

When Will returns to the table, he's carrying his coffee and motions to a stand in the back. "You can get water over there," he gestures.

This is unlike any date Julie's ever been on before. "Changed my mind," she says resolutely. "I don't need anything."

They exchange a few pleasantries, and Julie decides to move forward and ask the big question before she leaves.

"So, why aren't you in a relationship?" she asks him.

He looks into the air and says, "I'm really more of a lone wolf. I value freedom above all else and I haven't met anyone who's made me want to change that."

"What else do you value?"

He strums his fingers on the table as if he's agitated and answers, "A hot babe and a cold beer on a hot night." He laughs.

"I meant in life. What do you value in life?"

"That *is* what I value in life. That and a few other things," he says smugly.

She rolls her eyes. "Okay, it's time for me to go now," she gets up and grabs her bag. "Have a great night, Will." She walks away from the table. He doesn't say anything, just watches her as if it's the most normal experience in the world.

When she gets out to her car, she texts Jolene, "You won't believe the coffee date I just had." As she sends it, another text comes in. It's from Will.

"Let me make it up to you with dinner. Friday night. Your choice."

Sixteen

"Why are you putting makeup on, Julie? Aren't you just going to work out?" asks Nick.

"Yes, but I want to look sexy for Will, we're going out to dinner afterward" Julie responds with vulnerability in her voice.

Nick looks at her with compassion. "Oh, you can't help but look sexy. Besides, if he can't appreciate your naked face, he doesn't deserve your naked body."

Julie stops putting her mascara on and turns to look at him. "Aw, that's so sweet of you to say, Nick. Thank you."

She smiles at him and turns back to the mirror.

"Besides, I thought you didn't like this guy? Wasn't he late for your 'coffee date' and then acted like an evasive ass when you tried to have a normal conversation with him?" Nick asks.

She turns back around to face him. "Yes, all of those things are true. But, I haven't been on a date for so long and no one else has asked me. And he's been sending me really sweet texts ever since." She shrugs her shoulders and goes back to putting her lipstick on.

"Just be careful . . . he's a wolf in dog's clothing," he teases.

After her workout, Julie is in the gym restroom reapplying her lipstick and curling her eyelashes. *I never thought I'd be one of those women who wears a full face of makeup to the gym. I want to look my best for my date tonight and didn't want to sacrifice my workout. Maybe all of the other women wearing makeup here are in the same boat . . . somewhere important to go before or after the gym.*

She dabs her neck and chest with a towel and sprays a little perfume. *Hopefully that'll do the trick.*

She meets Will at the address he texted her, a swanky new restaurant bar in Beverly Hills. It's a trendy hot spot, one of those places to be seen. Pulling up to the valet in her car, she immediately feels out of place next to the fancy, expensive sports cars in line ahead of her.

When she gets out of the car, she goes into the restaurant. Will hasn't arrived yet. *Ugh. I'm so tired of waiting for Will.* There's no place to sit inside. It's very loud and crowded, so she escapes out the front door and waits near the valet stand.

Will pulls up thirteen minutes late in a sporty red convertible. *Figures.* He's dressed to the nines with black leather pants and his dress shirt unbuttoned halfway down his muscular chest. A gold chain peeks through the gap. He's built, but looks like a cartoon character in that outfit. *This guy seems to be all about appearances. I wonder what's going on inside.*

He greets her with a quick hug, and they enter the restaurant. The lighting is very dark and sensuous. It's so dim that she can barely read the menu. *I'll just ask for their recommendations . . . it'll be easier.*

Will sits next to her at the table and immediately puts one of his bear paws on her leg when he comes over. She lifts his hand and moves it back to his own lap. He spends a great deal of time looking around to see if he recognizes anyone. He tells her several times that this is "the place to be," where all the celebs hang out.

Julie feels alone amidst the crowd. It seems like a lot of style but very little substance and actual human connection. She decides to make the best of it and try to have fun despite her discomfort.

When the young blonde waitress comes by, Will looks her up and down and calls her "sweetie." *She must be at least twenty years younger than him. Poor girl having to try to make a living around these piranhas disguised as grown men.*

Julie is lost in her thoughts when she realizes that Will has ordered them cocktails without even asking her what she would like. When the martini arrives at the table, she politely explains to him that she doesn't drink hard alcohol.

"One drink isn't going to kill you," he says confidently.

Nick would never try to get me to drink something I didn't want. He's so insensitive. The macho man bullshit is tiresome. It's weakness masquerading as strength. This could be good inspiration for my novel.

Cake in Bed

Julie is feeling bored when Will catches her off guard and plants a big wet kiss on her mouth. At first she feels really awkward being kissed so publicly in the restaurant, but the kiss is so spine-tingling that she stops caring what other people might think and thoroughly enjoys it.

Wow. Our chemistry is off the charts. Maybe there's more to this guy than I thought.

Seventeen

"Oh my God, Nick! You won't believe it!" Julie sings into the phone.

"What happened?"

"I got the house! The big one, the dream one that we toured a few weeks ago. I put an offer in and my agent just called . . . it's mine!" She dances around while sharing the good news.

"That's wonderful, Julie. I'm so happy for you. Congratulations!"

"I'm so happy too!"

"Let's celebrate this weekend . . . how about you join me and Allison for a jazz brunch on Sunday?"

"Sounds perfect. Thanks, Nick."

Julie arrives at the restaurant for the jazz brunch wearing a lemon yellow sundress and a big smile. She sees Nick waiting out front and runs over to him with open arms. He gives her a huge hug, spinning her around.

"Hi, beautiful!" he says as he kisses her on the cheek.

"It's so good to see you!" she says, looking around. "Where's Allison?"

"Uh . . . she said she had a client to take care of and couldn't make it."

"Oh, okay. No worries . . . that's just more jazz and more brunch for us!"

He leads her through the restaurant and to their table in the sunlight.

"Wow. This is a really nice place," she says as he pulls out her chair.

"I love your dress, Julie. That color is so beautiful with your eyes." He smiles. "So tell me about your new place. When are you moving in?"

"I can't wait! I'd like to move in by the end of this month. I just need to sign all of the paperwork tomorrow and then book the movers."

"Movers? You don't have that much stuff. Why don't you let me help you?" he suggests.

"It's okay . . . I don't want to inconvenience you, Nick."

"I would love to help you."

"Well, Will said he would help."

"Then I definitely should be there. Are you still seeing him? How's it going?" he asks while pouring her a glass of orange juice from the carafe on the table.

She clinks her glass against his and takes a sip. "Um . . . I'm not sure. We've been on a few actual dates, but mostly we text back and forth. He calls me a lot and always seems to want to know what's happening in my world. I don't really mind, but sometimes it's a little weird that he wants to be close but from such a distance."

"Have you been intimate with him?" he asks quietly.

"No, he tries every time I see him, but I've told him that I want to move slowly and get to know his mind before I get to know his body."

"Smart. Good for you, Julie. You deserve a man who's in it to win it . . . not just in the bedroom, but in life."

"Thanks," she smiles and takes another sip of her juice.

"So just let me know what day and I'll be there to help you move. I mean it."

"Okay, I'll let you know. What's new with you?"

"Business is good. I guess everything's pretty much the same as usual," he laughs a little uncomfortably.

The jazz band comes pouring into the room with their saxophone, trumpet, and trombone as they get swept up in the music and celebration.

"I'm so grateful you guys came over to help me move today," Julie says as she hands Nick and Will bottles of water.

"Seeing you move into your dream home? I wouldn't miss it," says Nick.

Will grunts as he sits on the stairs of her front porch.

Julie sits on the porch swing with Nick and feels the breeze on her face and through her hair. "Can you smell the ocean air?" she asks with her eyes closed, lost in the moment.

"Yeah, it smells like fish and dirt," Will says flatly.

She ignores him and continues swaying in the breeze. She leans over and lays her head on Nick's shoulder next to her on the swing. He smiles and puts his arm around her.

Will looks over at them. "It's getting chilly. Why don't we go inside, Julie?" he asks as he walks over to the door.

"No thanks, I'm comfortable right here," she responds without opening her eyes.

Nick smiles at him and he begrudgingly goes inside alone.

"You did it, Julie," Nick says. "I know how hard you've worked and how badly you wanted a home of your own. And now you have it!"

She opens her eyes and looks up at him with gratitude.

Will opens the front door and comes back out onto the porch with a beer in his hand. He lets the door slam loudly as it's caught in the wind.

"It's starting to get dark. I don't have any food here since my refrigerator comes tomorrow. I guess you guys will be leaving soon to eat dinner," she says now that Will has disrupted their beautiful moment.

"Let me order a pizza for us, Julie. I don't want you surrounded by boxes with nothing to eat," Nick says as he grabs his phone.

"That sounds good to me. Would you like to stay for pizza, Will?"

"I think I should stay for dinner and make sure you're comfortable in your new place overnight," he says with a smile.

"Oh, that won't be necessary," she says, blushing.

"I insist," he says flirtatiously.

"Great idea," says Nick. "We should all stay and help Julie assemble her furniture tonight." He looks at her with searching eyes.

"Well . . . okay, guys . . . if you really want to stay, I guess that's fine. I don't have anywhere comfortable for you to sleep yet."

"I'm perfectly comfortable on the floor," says Nick. "I'll order the pizza right now."

After dinner, Nick is cleaning up the kitchen and goes into the bathroom. While he's in there, Will leads Julie into her bedroom to "show her something."

"Come over here," purrs Will with a devilish look in his eyes. "I know what you need. I want to give it to you." He looks her up and down. He's standing so close to her that she can smell him. A combination of sweat, stagnant cologne, and leather fills the air around him. His intensity feels intoxicating.

He pulls her ponytail down exposing her neck and gently but strongly kisses her collarbone. "Do you want me?" he asks seductively. She audibly gasps against her will.

Will looks over her shoulder through the half-open bedroom door and his eyes meet Nick's steely gaze. Nick's jaw is clenched and Will can tell that this show is getting to him. He smirks.

He takes her head in his massive hands and plunges his tongue into her mouth like an animal in heat. Before she catches her breath, she's on the bare mattress with his hands exploring her body.

She briefly thinks about asking him to stop, but it feels so good. He's irresistibly sexy.

Now on top of her, he takes off his shirt and flings it across the empty room as his beautiful body beckons her. Julie's fingers trace the carved lines in his chest and abs, his sweat glistening in his chiseled indentations. His body is a sculpted work of art.

Will turns and peeks out the door at Nick, who's fuming but speechless. Will smiles and raises his eyebrows as if to say, "Well, the best man won and now I get the award all to myself." He closes the door and continues to turn on the charm.

He returns to her on the bed and pushes his muscular chest up against her body. It's getting hot. Feeling him against her is making her want him so badly it feels like she may burst into flames.

He kisses her deeply, passionately, like out of a hot love scene in a movie. She feels his warm hands stealthily unhook and remove her bra on the first try. She thinks for a moment about how many bras he must've removed in order to become such an expert, but quickly loses her train of thought when she feels his magnificent hands on her exposed breasts. He's thrusting her with his hips and she can feel his enormous manhood pulsing against her.

He hungrily kisses her mouth, her neck, her breasts, and her belly, like a starving man who just received bread. He pulls her yoga pants and panties down with one, quick, forceful yank and she's lying there, naked, vulnerable, and wanting him intensely.

He looks up and smiles a wicked smile before spreading her legs wide open and plunging into her face first. He licks and sucks and then pulls away. "Your pussy is amazing. I love the way you taste." Kissing her again, he mumbles, "I knew you would taste good."

He then rubs his finger around the perimeter and deeply plunges his thumb into her body as far as it will go. She moans with pleasure but remembers that Nick is in the house and muffles her sounds with a pillow over her mouth.

Will sees her squelching her desire and grabs the pillow away from her. "No, I want to hear you," he says to her authoritatively.

Back to her mouth, he kisses her hard while unbuttoning his pants. She hears the tantalizing sound of his zipper going down and feels excited to see what's hiding underneath. He quickly and confidently kicks his pants and boxer briefs off onto the floor.

He stands up and proudly displays his manhood in his hands and proclaims, "Now you're going to get everything you need. Are you ready?" he asks with a sexy smile.

Before she can respond, he leans down to her and puts his hands on her hips. "Turn over," he says.

Confused, she asks, "What?"

"You heard me, turn over. Get on your knees," he says as his hands guide her hips around.

Julie's shocked and turned on at the same time. She obeys his instructions, longing for what could happen next. It's been a long time since she's had sex, and she's never been with a man who's so assertive in the bedroom.

"Okay without a condom?" he says as he lines himself up to enter her quivering body.

"No, that's a deal-breaker," she says, moving forward out of his reach.

"Fine, but it would feel better for you without this thing in the way," he says, digging into his pants lying on the bed.

He pulls something out of his pants pocket. She watches him roll a condom on. Then he pulls her hips back into position.

"You have a hot ass. I'm going to love fucking you," he says smugly. She's so turned on and wants it too badly to say anything about it. He smells so good. His body heat is radiating beside her. She wants to feel him behind her, inside her, all over her.

He pushes his hot, wet tongue against her while spreading her with his thumbs. It feels incredible. She arches her back into his mouth. "You're ready now."

He pulls his mouth away and replaces it with his huge, throbbing dick. Stretching her open and fingering her clit, he pushes the huge head inside slowly. "This might hurt a little bit at first, but you'll love it."

Will grabs her hips and thrusts all the way in fast and hard. She can't resist him even though she feels a little pain at first. He moans appreciatively, "God, you're so tight."

He controls her body with every thrust, every pull of her into him. His large, warm hands hold her into position as he rams her from behind.

She can't control herself anymore. She's moaning passionately, loudly, and so is he. She tries once again to muffle her moans with a pillow. He grabs the pillow and tosses it across the room. "No, I want to hear you," he says forcefully.

His sweat drips onto her back. He cums quickly. She feels the ripples throughout her body.

To her surprise, he stays inside pulsating for another minute. He pushes her head and shoulders down toward the bed. "Rest here for a minute or two. You'll need it."

He pulls out of her and says, "That was great, but this will be even better." He removes the condom and opens another one, ready to go again within minutes. Exhausted, she stays in position and rests for a moment.

She's shocked when she feels the tip of his penis against her ass. "Have you ever had it like this before?"

She gasps and quietly replies, "No."

"A virgin . . . I love it," he says with devilish delight.

Fingering her and spreading her open, he glides all the way inside. Slowly on the way in and quickly on the way out. He groans with pleasure. She feels the intensity, his weight against her, the intoxicating combination of pleasure and pain. It feels good and very naughty at the same time.

"Cum for me," he says loudly, dominating her body and her thoughts. He starts pounding her harder and his fingers flick faster. "Cum for me right now with my dick in your ass."

She feels a combination of ecstasy and embarrassment as she acquiesces to his commands. Panting and moaning so loudly, it's intensely sexy as she feels the release echo throughout her body.

Exhausted, she collapses beneath him onto the bed. He pulls out slowly, gets up, and saunters into the bathroom.

Alone for a few minutes, she catches her breath.

She rolls over onto her back and watches his sexy body strut back over to the bed.

"Are you ready for more?" he asks with a devilish laugh.

"I don't know if I can take it," she replies honestly.

"That's part of the fun of it," he says as he smiles and rolls a fresh condom onto his naked penis.

"Oh God, you have a gorgeous body," she says. He smiles smugly as he pulls her closer to him, lifting her legs up and placing them on his shoulders.

She's sore now and feels every inch of his entry but can't deny him. He gyrates his hips at the perfect rhythm and looks so sexy in the moonlight.

Before she knows it, she's cumming again and feeling the intense aftershocks ripple throughout her body.

"I stretched you out today. That pretty little pussy will never be the same," he declares while heading to the bathroom to clean up.

Julie reaches for him when he returns, wanting to kiss and feel the closeness of the intimacy beyond sex. He pulls away. "I only kiss and cuddle when it's leading to fucking. I'm done fucking for tonight, but maybe I'll fuck you again in the morning . . . if you're good."

He plops down on the opposite side of the mattress with his back facing her and quickly conks out. Still reveling in the ecstasy of their sexy rendezvous, she hears him start snoring like a bear and is quickly awakened from her trance.

She feels sexually satisfied in a brand new way, but hungry for connection. Will is snoring, and Julie is alone with her thoughts. Maybe this doesn't mean what she was hoping. She decides to just let it go for tonight and get some sleep. Maybe Will was right. Maybe all she really needed was a good fuck.

Eighteen

After a sleepless night desperately trying to forget what he heard, Nick lies on the living room floor. He can't stop thinking about what happened the night before. *Maybe I should've interrupted? No, Julie's a grown woman and can make her own decisions. I just hate to see anyone take advantage of her,* he thinks to himself while getting dressed. He walks into the kitchen to make some breakfast.

Will is already awake, strutting around Julie's new kitchen on the phone in his lime green briefs and flip-flops like he owns the place. Nick gives him the casual nod but is secretly burning inside. Will is talking to someone on his phone but acknowledges Nick with a half nod.

"Oh my God," Will says into the phone with his back to Nick. "You should see her tits . . . and that ass!" Nick gives him a disgusted look and leaves the room. After he finishes his call, Will walks into the living room and says, "I saw that look. Don't worry, I wasn't talking about her." He gives a smug grin and walks away.

Nick can't believe what he's hearing. Intoxicated by an anger-fear-jealousy cocktail, he wants to hurt this man.

He follows him into the kitchen. "Yeah, it takes a real man to lie to a woman to get her into bed with him." Nick scowls at Will and keeps his voice low. "Julie is a very special woman, not like the other girls you've been with. You don't love her, and you certainly don't deserve her . . . not even for a moment."

Will looks at Nick with facetious curiosity. "What do you care? Last time I checked, you're in a relationship." Will smirks as Nick's eyes burn holes in him. "I'll fuck whoever I want to fuck."

"If you hurt her . . ." Nick says, fuming. "How about you at least treat her with some respect while you're in her home?"

Julie bounces into the room and happily sings, "Good morning, guys!"

Nick turns and smiles at her. "Good morning, Jules," he says and tries to put their conversation out of his mind for the moment.

Will grumbles, "Morning," as he gulps down coffee.

Julie goes over to Will and kisses him quickly on the cheek. Will keeps his eyes fixed over her shoulder on Nick and then gives a little grin when he sees the anger burning in Nick's eyes.

Will puts one of his massive hands on her ass and squeezes it hard. Nick tightens his jaw and looks away. He feels sick watching Will manhandle Julie, but doesn't want to leave him alone with her. He feels an overwhelming need to protect her, especially from predators like Will.

He decides to change the subject. "So, what would you like us to set up for you first today, Julie?"

"Oh, I would love to sleep in an assembled bed tonight!" She smiles playfully.

Nick starts making eggs. He says, "Great, we'll get started after breakfast. Right, Will?"

Will shakes his head emphatically. "Not today. I'm out after breakfast. Will has important things to do."

Julie looks at him with surprise. She can't help but feel a little disappointed that he's leaving so quickly when they shared such an intimate night.

Nick says under his breath, "No surprise." He finishes making eggs for everyone and brings them over to the table where Julie and Will are sitting.

Will takes one look at the eggs on his plate and sneers, "I don't like sunny-side-up eggs."

Nick looks at him with calm incredulity and responds, "They are Julie's favorite eggs. I don't care if you eat them or not." Will begrudgingly takes the plate with a roll of his eyes.

Julie graciously accepts Nick's food and enjoys her eggs despite the tension at the table. She feels disappointed that Will isn't going to help and that he isn't acting politely at all toward her and her best friend. All she can think about is talking with Nick and getting his advice on this situation.

The three of them sit at the table eating breakfast in silence. There's awkwardness in the air. Julie doesn't know what to say, so she just eats her eggs, and Nick excuses himself to use the restroom.

After he finishes eating, Will stands up, leaving his dirty plate and fork on the table.

He stretches with a yawn and proclaims, "Will's gotta get dressed and be going now. See ya." Julie looks at him in surprise. *How could he leave so quickly without really saying goodbye after the night we shared?* She hears the bedroom door slam and feels ashamed.

Nick comes back into the room. "Where's Will?"

She doesn't have a chance to respond before Will walks back into the kitchen with his clothes on. She feels relieved for a moment, thinking that he realized he wants to kiss her properly. Her hopes are dashed as he reaches past her to grab his phone from the table. He senses the disappointment in her and wants to put on a little show in front of Nick. He decides to be benevolent and throw her a bone by leaning over and giving her a quick kiss while making a loud "mah!" sound.

Feeling emptier than she did before the kiss (she hates loud, dramatic kisses) and watching him walk out the door for a second time, she feels a pang of regret at having slept with him the night before. She brushes it off as best she can and focuses on cleaning up the dishes while Nick finishes his eggs. Frustrated with Will's behavior and sensing her disappointment, he gives her space.

"So, how are you feeling about last night?" Nick asks as he pulls all the pieces of Julie's bed together in her bedroom for assembly.

"Um . . . it was a fun night," she says coyly.

"Are you okay?" he asks as he starts putting together the headboard.

"What do you mean?"

"It's just . . . well, you know how Will is. And it sounded a little bit like an animal in pain at some point."

Julie's face turns bright red. "Oh my God, you could hear?" She feels mortified.

He gives a little closed-mouth smile and shrug of the shoulders.

"I'm so embarrassed," she says and looks away from him.

Nick puts the tools down and goes over to her. He touches her shoulder and turns her around to face him. "Hey, you've got nothing to be ashamed of. You're a red-blooded woman, and you hadn't had sex in a really long time. I'm not judging you, I'm just concerned about your well-being," he says gently.

She hugs him. "It's okay," he tells her, "just watch out for that guy. Now, let's get this bed assembled!"

They go back to putting the pieces together, her holding them in place while he screws them in.

Nick is quiet while he's focusing on their project. After a bit, he says, "Julie, there are a few things that I wanted to get your opinion on . . ."

She looks up at him. "Sure."

"This is a big one: I'm thinking about selling my company." He takes a deep breath. "There's an offer on the table and it's a very good one. If I take it, I would be set financially for at least five years, could take a little time off, and would be able to start a new company and build it from the ground up."

"That sounds amazing, Nick! You've built the business you acquired a few years ago, and I know you can build another one. You have a wonderful reputation in your industry. And you haven't really taken any time off for yourself in the years that I've known you. I think that could be time well-invested in your future."

He thinks for a moment and sits down on the mattress on the floor. She can see hesitation in his eyes.

"Why wouldn't you?" she asks as she sits next to him.

"Well, I tried to talk with Allison about it, but she thinks it's a bad idea. She said that I would be throwing away all of my hard work, and that because I've never built a business from the beginning before, my chances of success are very low."

He looks down at the ground between his feet. "She also said that if I take time away between businesses that people will forget who I am and I'll have to work five times harder to build the new business when I come back." He exhales loudly.

"Sorry, Nick, but she obviously doesn't know who she's talking to," she says seriously.

"I've been giving it a lot of thought lately, and I feel like I need to make some changes in my life."

Julie listens and puts her arm around his shoulders.

"I understand. What do you want to do?"

He looks over at her longingly and then looks back at the ground. "Honestly, I want to sell the company, take some time for myself to travel and do some soul-searching, and build a new architecture firm that's different, better than anything I've seen before."

She smiles and squeezes his shoulder. "There's your answer. That sounds more like the Nick I know! I know you can do it and that you'll be so glad you took the leap. I believe in you."

He smiles at her with deep appreciation in his eyes. "It feels good to talk with you about these things. I feel like I can be completely open with you."

"I'm always here for you to talk about anything."

"There's one more big thing," he says while he stands up and takes her hand to pull her up from the mattress. "But let's get this mattress onto your bed first."

They lift from their respective sides and get the box spring and mattress in place. Then, he helps her make the bed. As they pull up the comforter, Julie says, "I've never made a bed with a man before," with surprise in her voice. "I just realized that." She looks at him and laughs.

He smiles. "Actually, now that I'm thinking about it, this is the first time I've made a bed with a woman."

They both laugh and sit on the bed. "Feels a little scandalous," she says with a giggle. She looks at him seriously now and says, "Tell me the second thing, Nick."

He takes a deep breath and plays with her fingers beside him. "I'm breaking up with Allison."

She feels a little leap in her stomach. She definitely wasn't expecting to hear that. Electric waves pulse through her body, but she tries to stay calm and present for him.

"She just isn't my dream girl, and I feel our relationship has run its course. When she said all the reasons why I shouldn't go for my new business, I realized that she doesn't believe in me. She seemed more concerned with her own convenience than supporting me building my dream."

"Well, you know what's best for you, Nick."

"I don't like the way our communication has been lately. Maybe it's always been that way, and I just didn't notice it until now. We haven't been intimate in months. She always has something better to do."

"I'm sorry. I know that's disappointing. You're an amazing man, and you deserve someone who values and believes in you."

Nick looks at her and smiles. "And, she told me the other night that she never liked you."

She squishes up her face at his revelation and says, "I wonder why she would say something like that?"

He looks at her again. "I think she may be jealous of the connection that we share. That, or she's a bad judge of character. Either way, you're my best friend, and the person I'm with needs to respect our friendship."

"You have my full support in whatever you choose to do," she says in a measured tone. She is happy for Nick, but feels something else, too—excitement?

"What else can I help you with today?" he asks with relief in his voice, breaking up her thoughts.

"You've already done so much for me, Nick. Thank you! Now go enjoy the rest of your weekend." She laughs, gives him a hug, and goes to start unpacking boxes.

He follows her. "Are you sure you're okay? I'll stay with you if you want me to."

"I'm a little confused about the Will situation, but other than that, I'm good." She flashes an uncertain smile and goes back to her unpacking.

Nick walks over to her and takes her hands, looking her deep into her eyes. "Julie, nothing that guy says or does has anything to do with you. He's a pig, and he was lucky to get to be with you for a night. Don't throw away your celebration worrying about Mr. Muscles."

He laughs a little and continues, "I'm so proud of you for signing your deal and getting your dream home. You're amazing and you deserve it!"

He kisses her on her forehead and walks toward the front door. "I'll talk with you soon. Call me if you need anything." He smiles.

"Thanks," she says, beaming.

Nineteen

Julie's working out at the gym a few days later when she hears her phone ring. She pulls it out of her gym bag ready to press Ignore until she sees Nick's smiling face show up. She smiles and answers it right away. "Hey Nick!"

"How are you, Jules?" he asks. Julie detects something different in his voice.

"I'm great. What's going on?"

"Well, something happened to my eyes last night. It's not a big deal, but I need to go to the eye doctor, and he's telling me that I can't drive myself . . . you know I hate to ask for favors, especially when I know you're so busy . . ." he hesitates.

Julie can feel his discomfort and jumps in. "Are you okay? Are you at home? I'm already on my way." She packs up her gym bag and starts for the door.

"I'm fine. I just need to see the doctor soon. Sorry for the inconvenience. I really appreciate it."

"Of course, relax, and I'll be right there."

When Julie arrives at Nick's place, she knocks in her special way so he knows it's her.

She's surprised to be kept waiting at the door. Nick always runs downstairs, opens it immediately, and greets her with a hug right away, but not today.

She waits for a minute and then turns the doorknob. "Nick?" She enters slowly. "Nick, I'm here! Where are you?"

Nick comes slowly around the corner, wearing workout pants and a t-shirt, arms out in front of him, feeling his way along the wall. "Hi Julie! I'm so glad to *see* you," he laughs.

"Oh my God, Nick! You can't see!" she rushes over to him, notices his swollen eyes, and holds him in a strong hug.

"It's not that bad. It's temporary." He jokes and smiles but Julie knows him better than that.

"Are you ready to go now?" she asks, starting to tear up. She's never seen Nick in this state of pain before.

"Sure, do you want me to drive?" He laughs.

"Here, let me help you." She puts her arm around him and guides him through the door and into the car.

"Where is your doctor's office?" she asks a little panicked, realizing that he can't see to direct her.

"It's in my phone." He pulls his phone out of his pocket and holds it in his open hand for her. "The password is 2277."

She reaches for his phone. "Those are our lucky numbers."

"I know." He smiles. "That's why it's so easy to remember."

She gets the address and drives as quickly and calmly as she can. "What happened, Nick? Can you see anything?"

He reaches over, pats her knee, and says, "I'll tell you everything once we get there. Deal?"

She can see he's in a great deal of pain even though he's trying not to show it.

"Deal."

Once they arrive, she helps him out of the car, through the parking lot, and into the office waiting room. When they approach the front desk, the receptionist is unfazed. She gestures at the notepad and says that he's going to have to wait between appointments since he doesn't have an appointment.

Julie looks over at Nick sitting across the room, unable to see, eyes completely swollen and watering from the pain. She whispers to the receptionist, politely but firmly, "Do you see that man over there? He can't see anything and needs attention right away. If you don't see him now, he could go blind. It's a medical emergency."

The receptionist looks over at Nick and then looks back at Julie. "Let me see what we can do." Julie thanks her and goes to sit with Nick.

She's crying as she walks over, and he can't see her. She sits next to him on the couch. She grabs his hand and intertwines her fingers in his and lays her head on his shoulder.

"Julie, I have a confession . . . I'm a little scared right now," he whispers and holds her hand tightly.

"I know. It's okay, Nick." She rubs her thumb along his hand and holds back her tears.

"Nick?" the receptionist calls. "We're ready to see you now."

Julie helps him stand up and walks him to the office door. "I'll wait for you out here."

Nick asks sheepishly, "Would you mind coming in with me?"

She says, "Of course I'll go with you."

The doctor comes into the room. "Well, hello Nick. What's going on?"

Nick tells the story of what happened. "Hi Doc, this is kinda embarrassing . . . last night I was feeling a little self-conscious about the circles under my eyes. I decided to use some special eye cream my girlfriend left open on the bathroom counter just to see if it would make any difference. I rubbed it all over the area around my eyes and went to bed. When I woke up this morning, my eyes were burning and I couldn't see anything. I thought it would go away on its own, but it hasn't. I got scared and asked Julie to bring me to see you."

"Hmm. That's some powerful eye cream. Judging by the swelling, you're probably having an allergic reaction. Let's take a look."

Julie sits quietly during the testing. Nick's phone beeps in quick succession as he receives a series of text messages. "Anything urgent?" he asks. "Do you mind reading them to me, Julie?"

She glances at his messages and sees they're from Allison. She appears to be angry that he used her cream without asking. Julie is appalled but responds calmly, "Nothing urgent or important, Nick."

The doctor determines that he's having an allergic reaction to a non-FDA-approved ingredient in the cream. "I'm going to give you a prescription you can use for the pain. It should subside within forty-eight hours. The swelling will go down and you'll be able to see again in a few days."

"Thank God," says Nick with relief.

"But, you need to rest for the next forty-eight hours to make sure your vision returns. I'm serious. The risk of you going blind is very high if you don't listen. You need to be in bed with cold compresses over your eyes relaxing and keeping your blood pressure at a healthy level. Administer the drops into your eyes every four hours. No stress, no work, no exercise, no bullshit."

Nick takes a deep breath. "Okay, got it. Thank you for seeing me on such short notice."

"Get that prescription filled and go home and rest, Nick. Call me if you still can't see in three days."

Nick gets up to leave and runs right into the doorframe with a solid thud. He falls backwards a bit but catches himself on the table. "And please let your girlfriend help you," says the doctor.

Julie starts to correct him, but Nick didn't seem to mind the mistake. He's in too much pain.

His phone starts beeping again. She glances at the screen and sees more angry messages from Allison. "Nothing important," she assures him as she turns his phone off.

As she helps him to the car, she says, "I'm sorry you're going through this pain, Nick. I'm curious why you were feeling self-conscious of your face? You're incredibly handsome and that doesn't sound like you."

Nick gives a little embarrassed laugh. "Well, to tell you the truth, it's not like me to worry about silly things like that. But, last night Allison and I had an argument, and she said something about liking the younger pictures of me more than my recent ones. I know she was probably just trying to be hurtful, but I started to really obsess about my face and how much I'm aging. I just got curious and decided to try her miracle cream."

Julie listens as they drive to the pharmacy.

"This morning when I woke up and told her I was in pain, she flipped out about me using her products without asking her. She was so angry and I couldn't see what she was doing. She was yelling about me not caring enough about her and not getting out of bed when she was obviously so upset." Nick hangs his head.

"It was crazy. I still don't understand what was going on. I was shocked that she just left. That's when I managed to find my phone and to call you. Thank goodness for voice-activated dialing."

Julie parks at the pharmacy and grabs Nick's hand. "I'm so sorry, Nick. That sounds intense, especially in your current condition." He squeezes her hand back. "Let me run in and get your prescription for you. I'll be right back."

When they arrive back at Nick's place, he insists on carrying the pharmacy bag even though she has to lead him. "This bag is heavy, what kind of prescription did he give me?"

Julie laughs. "Well, I figured I might as well get you some sustenance while I was in there. I got your favorite protein bars, some of those green apples you love, and a box of those addictive crackers you like on treat day."

"You're a lifesaver, Julie!" he says and pulls her close to kiss her forehead.

Once they get inside, Julie helps Nick back to his bed and gives him the pain-relieving eye drops, which burn at first and then offer relief.

"I'm so grateful for your help this morning. What would I do without you, Julie?" he says sweetly.

"It's nice for me to be able to help you for a change," she laughs.

"You help me all the time," he says reassuringly. "I'll give you a call later."

"Nick, you can't manage on your own without being able to see. You'll hurt yourself . . . or starve, and that's not okay with me."

"I'll be fine," he says unconvincingly. "Maybe Allison will come by later."

"I'm not leaving you by yourself. I'll stay until she gets back."

"You don't have to do that. I don't want to disrupt your day."

Julie lays a cold compress across his eyes and puts a water bottle in his hand. "Oh thank you, I was getting so thirsty!" he says as he drinks the whole bottle.

"I know you were," she says gently.

"Come over here." He pats the bed beside him.

She takes off her shoes and crawls into his open arms. It feels so good to hold him and to be held by him. Seeing him so vulnerable makes her want to take care of him.

"How are you feeling, Nick?"

"Much better now, thanks to you." His voice drifts off a little at the end. He's falling asleep.

Julie lies beside him, and they drift off to sleep together.

When Julie awakens a few hours later, Nick is still asleep. She feels his warm body against hers. It's nice to be in the arms of a man she trusts. It's so comforting being in his bed. She looks up at him and studies his face. He's a very handsome man. And he smells so good.

His forehead is bruised from the encounter with the doorframe. He still looks dashingly handsome, even with the cold compresses over his eyes. He starts to moan as he rolls over. His hands meet her body, and he pulls her closer to him.

She feels the forbidden parts of his body press up against her. It feels so good being close to him. Suddenly, she feels hot imagining being with her best friend in a very intimate way . . . in his bed, with him blindfolded, both naked. Shocked at herself, she pulls away from him, gets out of bed, and goes to the bathroom to collect her thoughts.

She decides to distract herself by making dinner. Being as quiet as she can, she cooks a quick meal for them. She takes it into the bedroom for Nick. He's starting to stir a bit, but she can't tell if he's awake with his eyes covered. "Nick," she says softly, "are you awake?"

He turns his head toward her. "A little." He smiles. "My eyes are burning again."

She rushes over with the drops and refreshes the compresses. "Does it look bad?" he asks as his face is uncovered. His eyes are red and swollen shut as if two giant bees have stung him.

"No, it's not too bad, Nick. You still look handsome as ever." She smiles. "Hungry?"

"I'm starving."

"Good, because I made us some dinner."

"You're the absolute best!"

She hands it to Nick who immediately attempts to eat it while lying down in bed, making a huge mess all over his shirt and face.

When he's done, Julie asks if he wants help. He laughs. "Is it everywhere?"

"Pretty much." She laughs and tries to wipe the food off of his shirt to no avail. "You have a bunch of stuff on your shirt that won't come off."

"No problem." He sits up and starts to take his shirt off, but it gets stuck around the compresses around his head. He tugs and then falls backward, bumping the back of his head on the headboard.

"Looks like you could use a little help," she says as she moves in close and gently pulls his shirt over the compresses and off of his head. *God . . . he smells so good up close.* She quickly goes to grab another shirt for him.

"Is this okay, Julie? I'm much more comfortable now." She looks over at his shirtless body lying in bed, seeing the muscular ripples of his chest and indentations of his abs.

"Umm . . . sure."

"I think that medicine makes me tired or loopy . . . or both," he mumbles, grinning sleepily. "You really don't have to stay . . . but I like your company, and you're welcome to if you want to."

"I'm not going anywhere."

"Good. Do you wanna cuddle? I know you love cuddling," he says playfully.

"I like you tired and loopy." She laughs as she snuggles up next to him in his bed. It's gotten late, and she's starting to feel tired, too. All of that worry from earlier is catching up with her, and she's feeling emotionally and physically exhausted.

He laughs. "Do you know that I think of you all the time?" he asks while yawning as he's falling asleep.

He hugs her tighter against him. "Thank you for staying with me. You're an angel. There's no one I'd rather have here with me than you."

Julie is getting sleepy and doesn't respond.

Nick caresses her arm. "Julie? Are you awake?" he asks gently.

Barely conscious and so comfortable in his arms, she responds, "A little."

"Can I ask you something?" he whispers.

"Okay," she whispers back, keeping her eyes closed.

"What would you do right now if I were to kiss you?" he asks quietly.

She feels her stomach jump and her heart speed up. He continues to caress her arms. She feels the sexual tension between them envelop her and she feels out of control of herself.

"Have you ever thought about me like that?" he asks very vulnerably.

Julie looks up at his face in the moonlight. His mouth is open and he's feeling the same heat that she is. His body tenses a little. His heartbeat increases. She feels it against her body.

"Nick?"

"Yes?"

"I'm thinking about you right now." She slowly exhales as the words tumble out of her mouth.

"You are?" he asks hopefully.

"I can't help it."

"I wish I could see you," he says with a breathy smile.

She bravely rolls over on top of him, her legs straddling him, her face directly above his. She feels scared and on fire at the same time.

Nick takes a deep breath and puts his hands lovingly on her lower back. "Oh God, Julie." She feels him get hard beneath her. "I'm sorry. You're just so hot and sexy. Your body, your soul. I want you, Julie." He exhales audibly.

She touches his face lightly with her hand. She traces his lips as he kisses her finger. "I'm not going to be able to control myself much longer, Julie."

"Then kiss me." She hovers her mouth directly over his. She can feel the heat from his breath and can see the sweat on his face.

He takes a deep breath and then flips her over onto her back, his weight on top of her, his arms wrapped around her. He pauses a moment, his lips slightly open, his hardness pressed firmly against her special places. "I wish I could see your beautiful face and know what expression you're making. I don't want to do to the wrong thing here. I like you so much."

She pulls his body close with her legs wrapped around him. He pushes his hips against her firmly and rhythmically. Sweat is dripping onto her from his sexy bare chest. Her arms are wrapped around his hot, naked muscular back.

She gently raises her lips to barely meet his, showing him it's okay. "I'm going to kiss you now, Julie. If you want me to stop, I will. Just tell me, but I hope you won't want me to stop." They both take a deep breath in.

He licks his lips and presses them down to meet hers, slowly at first, and then more forcefully. His lips open her lips and his tongue explores the perimeter of her mouth before moving inside and finding her tongue to dance with.

They both feel the incredible sparks fly as their mouths meet. They kiss for several minutes that go by like seconds.

He places her hand on his bare chest and her fingers explore his sexy body. Barely able to catch her breath and desperately trying to control herself, she says, "Nick, this is amazing, but we need to get to sleep."

"Oh, you're right. I didn't mean to rush you. I adore you, Julie. I would never do anything to hurt you. I'm sorry I got carried away." He rolls over onto his back and takes several deep breaths.

"I'm not upset, Nick. I just don't want to take advantage of you in your current state." She giggles.

He laughs. "That was incredibly hot. It's going to be hard to get to sleep."

"We'll manage," she says, curling up next to him with her arm around his abdomen. He hugs her tight, kisses her forehead, and says, "Thank you for everything. Sweet dreams."

And they fall asleep in each other's arms.

Twenty

Nick awakens in pain before dawn. He feels fire in his eyes and goes to touch them and realizes his arms are wrapped around a woman, but not the usual woman who's been in his bed on and off for the past few years. With the compresses around his face and the darkness in the room, he couldn't see even if he weren't temporarily blinded.

He feels almost like he's hung over, but without the spinning room and nausea. His head is full of fog. He moves his hand gently to touch this mysterious woman. He touches her head and caresses her hair. Suddenly he remembers last night . . . he thinks, "Oh my God, it's Julie!"

His heart starts racing as he tries to piece together what's happened. *Julie is in my bed. What did I say last night? What did we do?*

Julie makes a little half-asleep noise while she turns to face him in bed. Her arm falls around his abdomen. She's just starting to awaken and feels a warm body in bed next to her. Nick feels her hand touching his stomach and moving up to his chest as she remembers that she's sleeping in Nick's bed.

His body quivers as her fingertips skim his muscles. Suddenly she awakens and pulls her hand away. Nick says in a light voice, "Good morning, Julie."

"Morning, Nick," she responds sheepishly. "Sorry about that . . . I'm not used to waking up next to a man . . . and just remembered it was you," she says with an embarrassed laugh.

"Oh, that? Don't worry. I never mind you touching me," he chuckles a little. "How did you sleep?"

"Honestly? The best I have in weeks." She sits up in bed and remembers his medicine. "Oh my God, you're probably in so much pain right now." She quickly gets out of bed and brings his drops over.

"It's not too bad," Nick assures her.

"You forget how well I know you, Nick." She lifts up the compresses and puts the drops into his eyes. "This will only burn for a second."

He tenses up as the liquid flows into his eyes. She freshens the compresses and he gently grabs her hand. "Thank you, Julie. The medicine makes my eyes feel better but makes me feel out of my mind." He takes a deep breath.

"Did I say or do anything that made you uncomfortable last night?" He holds his breath and waits for her response.

She sits on the bed beside him. "What do you mean?"

He rubs her back lightly and says, "I never want to do anything that makes you uncomfortable."

"You asked me about sleeping with your shirt off, and I was fine with that. You've got nothing to worry about, Nick.

But, thanks for being so considerate." She leans forward and kisses him on the cheek.

She gets up and starts to walk away from the bed. Nick playfully grabs her fingers. "Julie, what do you remember from last night?"

She sits back down at his bedside and thinks. "Well, we ate an amazing, restaurant-quality dinner." She laughs. "You made a huge mess all over yourself." They both laugh. "Then we curled up and went to sleep. Why do you ask?"

Nick releases a sigh of relief and pulls her hand to his mouth to give it a little smooch. "I'm so happy to hear that. The perfect ending to a crazy day." He smiles.

"*You* are crazy, my friend. It's one of your best qualities," she laughs. "Now I'm going to go make us some breakfast. Then, I'll go home, get showered, go to a meeting, and be back to check on you this afternoon."

"You're the best, Julie."

Julie walks out of her meeting on cloud nine. It couldn't have gone any better if she had scripted it herself. All she can think about is how grateful she feels and how much she can't wait to share the news with Nick.

Driving to his place, she thinks about the night before. It was so hard sleeping next to him after she saw him without his shirt. She's seen him shirtless before at the beach, but there was something different about him last night. Just remembering it makes her heart beat faster.

She stops by his favorite restaurant and picks up dinner for the two of them. It feels really good to be able to help Nick after all the times he's helped her. She's excited to see him and hopes that he's feeling better this afternoon.

When she pulls into his driveway, she sees another car parked next to his. It's a white BMW, and she doesn't recognize it. She grabs the food from her passenger seat and walks up to his place. She's surprised to find that the door is cracked open. She knocks loudly on the door. "Nick?"

She knocks again. No answer. She slowly opens the door and enters cautiously. "Nick?" she calls out.

As she turns around the corner, Allison plows through the kitchen toward her with anger boiling in her eyes. "Hi, Allison! So good to see you—"

Allison cuts her off and says, "I don't know how you can be friends with a man who's that stubborn and inconsiderate," and marches right past Julie and out the door.

"Call me when you grow up!" she yells back at Nick and slams the door behind her.

Julie sets the food down on the table and walks down the hall into the bedroom. "Nick?"

Julie walks into the bedroom and sees Nick sitting on the side of the bed, head in his hands. His compresses are off and his eyes are still red and extremely swollen. The room is a mess.

"Are you okay, Nick?" Julie asks and walks over to him.

Nick turns toward her and stands. "Oh, Julie." He holds his arms out to hug her, but can't see where she is. She walks into his hug and they hold each other tightly.

"What happened?" she asks gently.

Still holding her against him, he says softly, "I don't really know, to tell you the truth." He kisses her on her forehead before sitting back down on the bed.

"Allison is very upset with me. She came in calling me lazy and yelling. You know I don't do name calling or yelling. I got up and tried to calm her down. When I did, I fell over a suitcase she had in the floor. I guess she was packing up the clothes she had here."

Julie listens compassionately and pats his hand. "Did you get hurt when you fell?"

"Not much. I'm okay. The weird thing is that she didn't even seem to notice. She just kept yelling."

"I'm sorry, Nick. Let's see your leg." He pulls up his pants leg to reveal a bloody gash and a bruise forming.

"Oh my goodness, I'll get a bandage." She goes into his bathroom and comes back with a few things to doctor his knee.

"She wanted me to go to some event tonight. I don't know why she hadn't mentioned it before now. I offered to go and do the best I could, but that wasn't good enough. She accused me of ignoring her. She was acting crazy and said I was faking it. I took the compresses off to show her my eyes. She just wouldn't listen to reason."

"How are you feeling now?"

"Confused and in pain," he says as he flings himself back on his bed.

"Let's put some more drops in your eyes to help with the pain. I'm here for you. I brought dinner from your favorite place, too."

She puts the drops into his eyes and he hugs her close to him. "Thank you for being the special person you are, Julie."

Julie takes a deep breath. "I'm always here for you, Nick. Why don't we get you a shower and then eat some dinner?"

"A shower would be great, but I can't see anything. I'm a bit of a hazard to myself right now," he laughs.

She thinks for a moment and then says, "Well, I could start the water for you, put your towel by the shower, and be nearby if you need anything. Let's go for it. You'll feel better afterward." She pats his leg reassuringly.

She rolls up out of the bed onto her feet and then pulls his hands to lift him up. The weight of his muscular body pulls her instantly down on top of him, knocking the wind out of him. They both laugh hysterically for a minute before standing.

When they are solidly on the floor, Nick hugs her and says, "Thanks for the laugh. I needed that." He feels her back and notices that she's wearing a silky dress. "Oh my gosh, I almost forgot that you had your big meeting today. I'm sorry, Julie, I was so wrapped up in my own drama. How'd it go?"

"It was so good, Nick! I'll tell you about it when we eat dinner," she says and smiles with a sparkle in her eyes.

"A cliffhanger!" Nick laughs. "I guess that's more incentive for me to take a quick shower."

Julie goes into the bathroom, starts the water, and hangs his towel on the hook by the shower curtain. "All set." She leads him from the bedroom into the bathroom.

He stands shirtless, sightless, and defenseless before her. She just looks at him admiringly. His chin has light stubble growing in and his chest and arms have goose bumps. For a moment, she sees not her best friend, but a very sexy, masculine man in front of her.

Facing him about an inch away from his lips, she leans forward and gently removes the compresses from his face.

"Am I still horror film worthy?" Nick asks jokingly but with vulnerability in his voice.

"You are way too pretty to be scary, Nick." He smiles and then touches her face, gently exploring it with his hands as if he's discovering new territory and wanting to memorize every aspect of the terrain. His fingertips tenderly touching her nose, her cheeks, her lips. She's never had her face touched so intimately like this by anyone before.

She takes a deep breath and closes her eyes while listening to the water run. She wants to remember this moment and the way it feels to be touched with deep appreciation.

"You're so beautiful, Julie. Even without seeing you, I feel how beautiful you are."

She touches his hands with hers, cupping around them and slowly removing them from her face. She stands on her tiptoes and gently kisses each of his swollen eyelids. He smiles, lets out a little sigh, and turns toward the shower.

Julie leaves the bathroom, closing the door behind her to give Nick some privacy. She goes into the kitchen to put their dinners onto plates. She thinks about that moment and feels her stomach flutter again. *What does it mean?*

So maybe she's attracted to her best friend, the one man she knows deep down she can trust in the world. The idea makes her deliciously uncomfortable. She distracts herself by focusing on arranging the plates.

She hears the water turn off and heats their dinners in the oven.

Nick comes around the corner with just a towel wrapped around his waist. She gasps out loud.

"Sorry, Julie, I forgot to get some clothes to put on," he says as he attempts to navigate his way through the kitchen.

She helps him down the hall and into the bedroom as she tries to fight back thoughts about how incredibly attractive he is, even with the swollen eyes. He's shockingly sexy and she can't stop checking him out. *Thank God he can't see me right now.*

In the bedroom, she asks where to get the clothes he wants to wear. "The drawer on the left has boxers and pants I can sleep in," he responds.

Julie opens the drawer and sees Nick's boxers and boxer briefs alongside some fleece cargo pants and a box of condoms.

She can't help but notice that the condoms are large, in assorted tropical colors, and are "ribbed for her pleasure."

She hands him a pair of black boxer briefs and the pants. "Thank you. I hope there's nothing embarrassing in that drawer," Nick says.

Julie chuckles. "Nothing I haven't seen before."

She leaves the room to get their dinners out of the oven. When she returns, Nick is wearing the boxer briefs and is bending over to put on his pants. His foot keeps getting caught in the leg and he falls over onto the bed.

"I can't believe I can't even put on my own pants," says Nick with a nervous laugh. "Now I'm really embarrassed."

"Don't be," she says. He stands up straight and puts his hands on her shoulders. Facing him, she leans down to grab the waist of his pants from the floor and help guide him into the legs.

As he stands there in his boxer briefs, she gazes at his solid physique. She has a hard time being that close to him when he has so few clothes on. She quickly pulls the pants up over his legs and butt and moves away. "Hot in here, isn't it?" she asks.

"Yes, that's the one thing I would change about this place . . . air conditioning. Thanks for your help, Julie."

He sits on the bed and she goes over to put some drops into his eyes. "Wait, you're wearing a fancy dress, aren't you?" he asks.

"A little fancy."

"I bet you look gorgeous and that you stunned them with your brilliance at your meeting today. You want something more comfortable to wear?"

She thinks for a moment. "That would be great, but I didn't bring any other clothes."

"You can wear one of my t-shirts. I have a really soft one in the top drawer."

She goes over to the dresser and finds it. "The black one on top?"

"That's the one. It's my favorite. Take it with you if you want." He grins.

"Okay, but I can't get my zipper down on my own." She laughs and stands in front of Nick with her backside toward him.

"I can fix that," says Nick as he feels for the zipper on the back of her dress. He holds her hip with one hand as he slowly unzips her with the other.

"Thank you," she says as she slips out of her silky pink dress and pulls his t-shirt on over her bra and panties. It's so soft it's almost silken on her skin. "That's much more comfortable."

Nick smiles.

Julie goes into the kitchen and pulls their warm plates out of the oven. She brings them into the bedroom and sits next to Nick in bed to eat.

"This is delicious," he says as he takes big spoonfuls of lobster macaroni into his mouth. "So thoughtful of you to do this for me. Thank you."

"I'm happy to do it, Nick."

They eat in a comfortable silence for a few minutes, both thinking about that moment right before Nick's shower. Then he says, "Tell me about your meeting today."

"Oh my God, Nick, it was amazing! They loved my ideas and we talked about moving forward with the next two books in the series! And, the offer was three times higher than I hoped it would be!" she gushes.

"That's wonderful, Julie! Wow! Congratulations! I can't wait to celebrate something else with you," Nick says, beaming. "All of your hard work is paying off."

"Thanks, Nick! It's exciting!"

They finish their dinners, and she washes the dishes. When she returns to the bedroom, Nick is lying in bed, seemingly lost deep in thought.

Julie sits by his bedside and puts his compresses back on. "How are you feeling?"

"Much better now thanks to you. My eyes feel okay. I think the medicine is kicking in. I'm a little tired."

He pauses for a moment and clears his throat. "Are you going to stay tonight?" She hears hopefulness in his voice.

"Would you like me to?" she asks, her voice lilting up.

"Will you judge me if I say yes?" He laughs a little awkwardly.

"For you, I'll stay . . . no judgment required." She turns the light out and crawls into bed beside him, lying on her back. Nick rolls to face her and puts his arm around her abdomen. He can smell the light vanilla scent of her hair and feel its softness against his cheek.

"Do you want to talk about what happened with Allison?" she asks. Nick breathes in and responds, "Not right now, but thank you." They lie together in silence for several minutes.

"I had a dream about you last night, Julie," Nick says hesitantly.

"What happened in the dream?" she whispers.

Nick thinks. "Um . . . I can't tell you."

"You can tell me anything."

"Not this."

"So, I'm guessing it was a bad dream?"

"No, it was a very, very good dream."

Julie smiles. "That's good . . . goodnight, Nick."

He snuggles her tighter. "Night, Julie."

Twenty-one

Julie wakes up with a loud gasp in the middle of the night. She sits up in bed, sweating and out of breath. Nick feels her move and instinctively wakes up. "Are you okay, Julie?" he whispers as he touches her back, which is wet.

"I was having a nightmare," she sputters out.

"Come here and I'll hold you while you tell me about it."

She curls back up with Nick. "I'm sweaty and disgusting." He rubs her back, which has soaked through his soft t-shirt. "Don't worry, you could never be disgusting."

In the safety of his arms, she shares the bad dream with him. "I dreamt that you died, Nick," she says as tears form in the corners of her eyes.

"It's okay, I'm here with you right now," he assures her and holds her tighter.

"It was terrible. I felt in that instant like I lost everything that mattered in my life," she weeps. "I've never felt sadness like that before. I thought I had, but I was mistaken."

He puts his hand around the back of her neck and head and pulls her closer to him.

"It was so intense and so real. I was heartbroken in a way I've never experienced." Her tears flow onto his bare chest.

She says honestly, "I don't know what I'd do if I ever lost you."

"I'll always be here for you. You don't have to worry, Julie. I'm fine. It was just a bad dream." He kisses her forehead and gently rubs the tears from her eyes.

Julie looks up at him, his face shining in the moonlight. She carefully removes the compresses from his eyes. The swelling has gone down. "Can you see me, Nick?"

He slowly opens his eyes. His eyelids feel so heavy and he still feels like he's hung over. "I can see you a little with my eyes. I can see you completely with my heart."

"What do you see?"

Nick touches her face gently with one hand. "I see the most incredibly beautiful, sexy, talented, wonderful woman in the world with a big heart and an adventurous spirit. I see an authentic person who uplifts and inspires people and who deserves the best in life and love."

Tears continue to flow lightly down Julie's cheeks and onto his chest. "You are my favorite person on the planet, Nick."

Under the covers, his toes play with her toes. Julie smiles. Nick smiles, too. He knows just the right things to say and do. She freshens the compresses on his eyes before laying her head onto his chest, and they fall back asleep.

Nick wakes up alone in bed. He slowly opens his eyes, gasping a little as the familiar shapes of his room return to focus. His eyes are a little sore, but they're working again. He slowly blinks as relief spreads through him.

Just then, Julie walks into the room. She's moving quietly to avoid waking him up. Nick watches her in the faint early morning sunlight, her hair wild from sleeping and her curves showing through his soft and clingy t-shirt that ends just above where her toned legs meet her round butt. He admires her femininity as she crawls back under the covers.

He reaches over and tickles her, catching her off-guard. "Good morning!" he laughs.

"Oh, Nick! You surprised me!" She tries to hold back her laughter but succumbs to his persistent tickles. She squirms and moves away only to roll over toward him again. "You're so sneaky!" she squeals. They both laugh wildly as they roll around in the bed.

"Let me see your eyes, Nick," she pleads, trying to squirm away from his playful grasp. "Never!" he says as he tickles her once more.

She rolls over facing him, nose to nose, and grabs his head around his ears. "Look at me." He complies and looks deep into her eyes for the first time in the past few days, and in another way, for the first time ever.

They both get quiet. "You look different," she says, the pitch of her voice rising with surprise.

"So do you," he whispers while staring intently at her.

He puts his hands on her shoulders and rubs her arms.

"Your eyes are so blue. It's wonderful to see them again, to see you again."

"My eyes have missed seeing you, too," he says tenderly.

"I'm so glad you're feeling better!" As she finishes the sentence, she realizes that he won't need her to stay anymore. Hesitating, she says, "I guess I'll get going now," and starts to turn over to get out of bed.

"Wait . . ." Nick says pleadingly and gently pulls her back toward him. "It's Sunday. Why don't we spend the day together? Now that I can see, I can make you banana pancakes. We can watch '80s cartoons."

She looks at him coyly. He smiles.

She sees the beautiful twinkle in his eyes, the thing that she missed the most over the past few days. "How can I say no to an invitation like that?"

"But first, cuddle?" he asks, pulling her toward him and wrapping his strong arms around her petite frame.

"I love your hugs, Nick." She snuggles her head into his neck, tucked under his chin.

"What a coincidence, I love hugging you," he says with a squeeze. "I can't thank you enough for what you've done for me over the past few days. Thank you for taking care of me." He kisses her on the forehead.

She smiles and closes her eyes, savoring the bliss of the moment in the arms of the man she most respects and adores.

A few days later, Nick is at the gym in the evening after leaving his office. He's taking turns spotting and being spotted by his friend Asa on the bench press.

"Did I tell you that Julie just signed a major book deal?" Nick asks Asa as he gets into position on the bench.

"You might've mentioned it a few times," Asa says with a chuckle.

"I'm just so proud of her!" he says with a smile.

Nick thinks out loud. "There's something about Julie. She's irresistible even when she's being ridiculous. She's the kind of woman you just can't stop thinking about and don't want to. Every move she makes is so uniquely her. You could spend all day in a parking lot with her doing nothing but talking and have the best day ever. I've never met anyone like her before, and I doubt I ever will again."

Asa loads the barbell and replies, "You know what they say about things you can't go a day without thinking about . . ."

"What?"

"That you should pursue them at all costs because they could be your destiny," Asa says with a smile.

"To tell you the truth, I want her so badly. But I'm afraid I'll fuck it up. I don't know if I could live with myself if I upset or lost her."

"Well, buddy, it seems to me that the only real way you could fuck it up is by not trying—not going for her. She could be the best thing to ever happen to you," Asa says as he spots him doing his reps.

Nick thinks for a moment and then responds with a grunt while lifting, "Julie is the best thing that's ever happened to me."

"What about Allison?"

He sets down the barbell, takes a deep breath, and exhales with gravity. "She's a good person . . . and I don't want to hurt her, but Julie may be my soul mate. Something happens when Julie touches me. I've never experienced that before. I'm going to break it off with Allison tonight. It's the right thing to do."

Asa smiles. "You're a good man, Nick. Go for Julie—you only lose if you don't play."

Nick gets up, and Asa gets onto the bench. "You're right. I can't imagine my life without her. I'm nervous, but I'm going to go for her anyway."

Asa puts his hand on Nick's shoulder. "Bro, life is short. If she makes you happy, you owe it to both of you to explore it. If you don't, you'll always wonder 'what if' and then you'll have to watch other men line up for her."

"Not cool, man."

He starts to lift and says, with a little laugh, "That motivates you, huh?!"

"You knew it would. You're a good friend. Thanks, man." He spots him while lifting.

"Keep me posted. I want a wedding invitation," Asa says with a mischievous smile.

"You're so funny."

Asa sets down the barbell and stares up at Nick. "Why are you still here? Go get her!"

Twenty-two

"Julie! Hey! I have big news . . . what are you doing tonight? Can I come over?" Nick asks over the phone.

"Hey Nick! I don't know if I can wait until tonight to hear your news . . . what are you doing right now?"

"I'm leaving my office and heading home. Where are you?"

"I'm writing at my café, and I just hit my word count for the day. Do you want to meet at the ocean and go for a walk and talk?"

"Sure, I'll just change clothes and see you shortly."

Nick arrives at the café thirty minutes later, looking dapper in his gym shorts and fitted athletic shirt. He sneaks up behind her and gives her a kiss on the cheek. "Julie!"

She turns around and gives him a big hug. "I have a feeling that I know what you're going to say," she says playfully.

He smiles ear to ear and helps her gather her laptop and notebooks. "Today is a big day for me. I can hardly wait to tell you."

They drop her bag off in her car, and he takes her hand as they walk down to the pier.

"So, how was your day?" he asks her.

She lightly smacks him on his chest. "Tell me already!" They both laugh.

"I sold my business to a very distinguished architecture firm from Australia today . . ."

"Oh my God, Nick! That's amazing! I'm thrilled for you!" She bounces up and down a little as they walk down the sidewalk.

"And . . . I broke up with Allison last night." He smiles.

"What? Wow! Congratulations. Big changes for you today! How are you feeling?"

"Like a huge weight has been lifted off of me." He grins. "And, I have a contracting deal with the firm to do a few projects in Australia next year."

They walk onto the pier and are followed by a pelican.

"That's wonderful. I'm proud of you! What does that mean for you right now?"

"Well, I'm a free man. I have the money to take some time off and start my own firm from the ground up whenever I'm ready."

"So amazing! You deserve it, Nick! And how did it go with Allison?"

"I did the right thing. After I had 'the talk' with her, she called me a bunch of names and then admitted that she's been cheating on me with one of her clients for the past few months."

"Oh my God, Nick! I'm so sorry," she says as she stops and hugs him.

He grips her tightly in return. "It's okay. I knew something was amiss—I wasn't ever in love with her. She brings so much drama to every situation. She's not like you. It's hard to admit, but I should've ended it a long time ago."

"Wow! Well, I'm blown away. I admire the way you take action so quickly once you've made a decision. So inspiring!"

They stop and sit on a bench overlooking the ocean. The sun shines gently on them as it begins to set.

"This is my favorite time of day, when the sun melts into the ocean," she says looking out into the water. He holds her hand as they gaze into the sunset.

"I have news . . . but not as big as your news," she laughs.

He looks at her with interest. "Tell me."

"I'm going on an overnight trip with Will this weekend, and he's going to meet my family," she says with a hint of disbelief in her voice.

"Really? Whose idea was that?"

"His, surprisingly enough," she says. She raises her eyebrows and shrugs her shoulders. "I figured, why not? You only live once, right?"

"The plot thickens," he says with a tease.

"Whoa! You're wearing that today?" Will asks with a tone that insinuates that she should not, in fact, wear that outfit today or ever again.

She looks in the mirror at her classy, form-fitting turquoise dress. "Yes, why do you ask?"

"It's just that you look too sexy," he pouts. "And if you're wearing that to my event today, no one will notice me or anyone else."

Julie looks over at him sitting on the bed while she's putting on her earrings. "Really, Will?"

"I don't think it's unreasonable to ask you to wear something more conservative. It's supposed to be my day."

"I love this dress, and I've worked really hard to have a fit body to wear nice clothes like this. No one is paying attention to me, anyway. I'm here to help make you the star today."

Deciding that he must be nervous about the event, she walks over to him on the bed and leans over to kiss him on the lips. He receives her kiss, but then pushes her away without returning it.

"I don't like you outshining me, Julie."

"I don't see what my dress has to do with anything. Why can't we shine together?" she asks honestly.

He grunts. "Fine. Wear whatever you want."

Taking a deep breath, she calmly responds, "I don't need your permission to wear anything, Will. I came out here with you to help at your event and that's what I intend to do. Putting me down isn't a way to express your appreciation, and I don't like it."

"I don't have time to debate this with you right now," he says while looking at his watch. "You're making me late. Thanks a lot."

He walks out the hotel room door and lets it slam behind him. Hesitating for a moment, she decides to grab her purse and follow him, wondering what's in store for them today. She never knows what she's going to get when she's with Will.

Sitting in the candy apple red sports convertible in the pouring rain after the event, Will informs Julie, "Before we go meet your family, we need to talk." Julie's heart sinks into her stomach as she listens for what will come next.

Will continues, "Obviously you've noticed that my behavior has been different today . . ."

"Yes, I definitely noticed that you're not yourself, you've been acting like a real asshole," she replies matter-of-factly.

He pauses for a moment, glaring at her. "I don't think that it's a good idea for me to meet your family. I'm not feeling 100% about this relationship. I'm not going."

"What? Are you serious?"

Will looks at her unapologetically. "Yep."

"What am I supposed to do? I'm hours away from home, and my family is expecting us for dinner . . . which was your idea to begin with! My mom is making all this food for us. Why are you doing this?"

"I feel trapped, and I don't really have time for a relationship. I just want to be free to be me," he says, looking away from her.

"You are unbelievable," she says, slowly sounding out every syllable.

"I figured it was good to let you know before getting your family involved. Plus, you deserve someone who's 100%."

"Hell yeah, I do! I don't have time for this confused little boy, Peter Pan bullshit, Will. I need to make a phone call," she says.

He looks at her coldly as he pulls out his phone. "Fine, go ahead," he replies gruffly.

"I would like to make a private call. Please get out of the car."

He looks offended and starts to open the car door. "Where are the keys? You're not going to drive away, are you?"

Julie looks at him incredulously. "Of course not. I'm not like that."

He reluctantly gets up, tells her, "Text me when you're done," and closes the car door behind him.

Feeling panicked, Julie calls the one person she knows she can always trust. The phone rings and rings before going to voicemail. She hears Nick's voice and leaves a frantic message. "Nick, something unexpected has happened, and I'm in a very difficult situation with Will. I don't know what to do. I'm about three hours away from home, and I have to make an important decision right now. I'm safe, but I need your help. Please call me back as soon as you get this. Thank you!"

She hangs her head, thinking about her next move. Obviously she doesn't want to spend any more time with Will, but she's so far from home without a backup plan. And her family is expecting them. Now she's going to have to explain to everyone that Will is a douche and broke her heart.

Her phone rings, and she picks up immediately. "Julie, just got your message. Sorry I missed your call. What's going on?" Nick asks with concern.

"Oh my God, Nick. You were right about Will. He just told me that he's not 100% in our relationship and that he's not going to meet my family. We're supposed to be having dinner with them in thirty minutes! Just last night he was telling me how much he loved me . . . I'm hungry and exhausted from helping Will with his photo shoot all day. And I honestly think he may be on drugs right now. His behavior has been so erratic over the past twenty-four hours. I feel really confused. I don't know what to do."

"I'm glad you called me. Everything's going to be okay. Where are you?"

"I'm in Cabazon . . . in the parking lot where the dinosaurs are."

"I'm leaving my office now and coming to get you. Is there anywhere safe you can go to get away from Will and wait for the next hour or so?"

She looks around. It's getting dark, and the rain is relentlessly streaming down from the sky. "Everything's closed here and it's raining like crazy in the desert. I'm scared, Nick."

"Here's what to do: stay in the car and insist that he stay with you until your ride comes. He's unstable. I don't trust him driving with you in the car. And I know you want to run away from him right now, but I don't want you waiting outside in the rain by yourself either." He takes a breath.

"Stay calm and keep him talking. Ask him the questions you want answers to. You are strong, beautiful, amazing, and way too good for him. He led you on. You deserve answers.

"Remaining calm will throw him off balance. He loves to talk about himself so he'll engage in the conversation. This is your time to be a peaceful warrior. Tell your family that you're going to be late. Sit tight—I'll be there as soon as I can.

"Oh, one more thing, when he sees how calm you are about it, he's likely to backpedal. Don't let him touch you or think that he has another chance with you. He'll just manipulate you in his game. Protect your physical, mental, and emotional space at all costs."

Julie takes a deep breath. "Okay, got it. Thank you so much, Nick."

"You don't deserve this bullshit. I'll be there to take care of you soon."

Twenty-three

Julie's pulse has slowed somewhat after talking to Nick. His careful instructions have brought her back down to earth. She regains her composure for a minute and then texts Will, "You can come back now."

He opens the car door and gets back in, soaking wet from the rain. "That took longer than I thought it would," he says smugly.

"Here's the plan . . . We're going to wait here for my ride, which will be here in about an hour."

"I can drive you somewhere and drop you off."

"No, we're waiting here. And now I need to call my mom to let her know I'm going to be late."

"Fine."

She calls with him in the car. Her mom is concerned, but Julie assures her that she's fine and will be there late. She tells everyone to go ahead and eat if they're hungry now. She'll see them in a few hours.

Once she hangs up with her mom, Will says, "I'm sorry to put you in the position to make that call. I know it wasn't easy."

Julie looks at this man who seduced her and swept her off her feet only to dump her on the floor after she helped him so much on his big day. "Why would you do this?" she asks calmly.

"Well, there wasn't a good time to tell you before . . ." he trails off. "You know, and, maybe I'm sabotaging myself in some way."

"You mean that you wanted me to work for you all day for free and then not have any responsibility. You needed my help and now that you don't, you feel fine just being the way you really are."

"Damn, you're cute," he says, "but you've got too much sass. And, you'd look better if you lost five pounds. As a matter of fact, if you could keep your mouth shut, you'd be a lot more attractive," he says, knowing that his words would hurt her.

She looks down for a moment and then directly into his eyes with disdain. "I was good to you, Will. I don't see what my independence and my weight have to do with anything. You may be intimidated by me, but the bottom line is, you're an asshole . . . you just told me right now." She stares at him intensely as if she can burn holes through him with her eyes and secretly wishes she could.

"Look, you're a really good person," he says, backpedaling, "and I'm not a very good person. You don't really know me. You bring out the best in me, and I love that about you. But that's not who I really am. And if you knew the real Will, you wouldn't like him."

His words are hurtful to her because she accepted him for who he was without putting pressure on him to be any different. But now he's starting to reveal more of himself, and she's remembering Nick's advice.

"Don't worry," he continues, "I'm still very attracted to you. You're the sexiest woman I've ever been with and we can still have sex if you want to. I'm not trying to cut you off, I just want to expand my options."

Julie feels sick. "Expand your options?"

"You know, be available to be with other people. To be free to do whatever I want with whoever I want . . . without the guilt." He looks really satisfied with himself in this moment. "So, do you want to keep having sex?" he asks while placing his giant hand on her thigh.

"Not with you," she responds coldly and pushes his hand away.

He looks shocked and she sees a hint of disappointment in his face. She looks out the passenger window, hoping that Nick will arrive soon. She feels disgusted and wonders what she ever saw in Will. All the muscles and good hair in the world can't make up for his entitlement complex.

The night is dark and the rain is so dense that she can't even see the giant dinosaurs outside her window.

He plays with his phone for a few minutes then says, "I'm not mad at you."

She looks over at him incredulously. "Good, because I haven't done anything to you."

He rolls his eyes regretfully. "Maybe I'm making the biggest mistake of my life right now, throwing away the one person who's actually good for me."

"Maybe," she says in a disinterested tone while going back to watching the rain roll down the windshield. "But you're not 'throwing me away,' I'm leaving you."

He reaches for her hand and tries to hold it. She loves the feeling of his skin against hers and would like the comfort, but quickly pulls her hand away and denies him. "Don't touch me. I'm done with you."

"Wait a minute . . . we can still be friends and go out and do stuff just for fun," he persists.

She looks him right in his beady eyes. "No, that wouldn't be fun for me. I am done wasting time on people who waste my time."

"Besides, you're barely scratched the surface of your potential. You need me to help bring out the greatness in you," he says confidently while picking his teeth with his fingernail.

"I don't think so, Will," she says flatly and pulls out her phone.

He sighs and shifts in his seat for a minute while she checks her texts. "Who's picking you up?" he asks with desperation.

"It's really none of your concern at this point," she says as she puts her ear buds in and closes her eyes to relax.

Through the rain-splashed window, Julie sees the lights of Nick's truck pull into the lot and park next to Will's car. She feels a huge sense of relief knowing that he's nearby and that this nightmare with Will is about to end.

She gathers her purse and her phone. Will looks at her like he's expecting a goodbye kiss. "Goodbye, Will," she says with as much courage and compassion as she can. She gets ready to open the door and Will grabs her shoulder.

"Hey, we can still be friends, right?" he asks chummily.

Julie looks him in the eye and says, "Nope." His jaw drops and he looks shocked. But not as shocked as he looks a moment later when Nick opens Julie's car door.

Nick offers Julie his hand to help her out of the car. He stands solidly in the rain and says nothing to Will, just gives him a stern look and then focuses completely on Julie. She gives him a quick hug. "I'm happy to see you," she says as she shivers at the touch of the cold rain.

"It's always wonderful to see you, Julie. Do you have anything else?" he asks as he closes the car door.

"A few bags in the trunk." He walks around to the back of the car. Much to Julie's surprise, Will gets out of the convertible and rushes around to manually open the trunk. "The stupid button doesn't work," he grumbles as he opens it with the key.

While jostling his keys around, he complains, "It's freezing out here in the rain and the wind," as he scampers back into the driver's seat.

Nick and Julie ignore him and get her bags into his truck. He walks her around to the passenger side and opens the door for her. When he gets into the truck, he takes a long look at her. She's sad and soaked, but not crying. Her heart has been broken, but she's not broken. He feels so much compassion, love, and admiration for her.

He starts the engine and pats her on her leg. "You are so strong. I'm proud of you for handling this situation so well. Everything's going to be okay," he says reassuringly. "And I brought you a snack to hold you over until we get to your mom's house." He hands her a protein bar and turns her seat heater on.

"You're the absolute best, Nick." She rips open the wrapper and takes a quick bite. She instinctively breaks the bar in half and hands him the other half. He looks at her, smiles, and silently accepts her gift. She savors the delicious smell of lemon in the air as she tries to warm up from the rain.

"So, how did it go in the car with him? Did he try to put any moves on you?" he asks in a concerned tone.

"It wasn't fun, but it was fine. He's a very fucked up person. I can't believe I didn't see it before. I so wanted to believe what he told me, but you were right, his audio never matched his video. It's disappointing because I was falling for the man he pretended to be. At least I know now who he really is. It hurts, though," she says as she starts to cry.

He pats her leg and gives her knee a firm but loving squeeze.

"I'm in shock. What's wrong with me, Nick? Why do I keep driving guys away?"

Watching the road but listening intently, he says, "There's nothing wrong with you. These guys are idiots. You are beautiful, smart, and amazing, and they just aren't used to that rare combination. They don't know what to do with you. It has nothing to do with you."

"Will actually had the nerve to tell me that I have too much sass and that I'd be a lot more attractive if I lost five pounds. I hate him." She starts to cry.

Agitated, Nick pulls over on the side of the road. He parks the truck, but keeps the engine running. He looks at Julie and gently reaches for her hands. "It's really important for you to hear this, Julie. There's nothing wrong with you. You are perfect exactly as you are. A real man would never ask you to be less than what you are."

Julie starts gasping with big tears flowing down her cheeks. "It's true, I have gained a few pounds, though."

"Please don't let that asshole bring you down. Your sparkling personality and beautiful, feminine body are breathtaking and so sexy. You've always been hot, and in my humble opinion, you look the best you've ever looked right now. He's just a loser and can't handle a woman like you. Small minds are like that. I hate that he did this to you." He wipes away her tears.

"I probably could lose a little more weight and then my body would be perfect."

Nick lifts her chin so that she's looking into his eyes. "Your body is perfect right here, right now. No changes required or desired. He's just talking shit to throw you off his path and make you feel like it's your fault. I assure you that it's not you."

She looks up at Nick, blinking through tears, and gently smiles before taking the last lemony bite of her half of the protein bar. "What does it all mean?"

"Julie, these guys don't deserve you, and that's the truth. They can't handle someone who really has their life together, someone on top of their game like you," he says and puts the truck into drive, navigating back onto the freeway.

"I just want to love and be loved for who I really am," she says with a sob.

"I know, and you will be by the right man. These other guys are just boys. Don't blame them for not knowing what to do with more when they're used to so much less. You deserve the best." Julie cries. He squeezes her leg, and his hand lingers there.

"Am I doomed to be alone, watching all the other happy couples walk by enjoying the fullness and beauty of life while I sit on the sidelines?" She gasps as big, round tears pour down her cheeks.

Nick looks at her and says with a smile, "Definitely not. You're just feeling sad right now and that's understandable. You're their 'if only' girl. If only they were more successful, if only they were more fit, if only they could keep up with you . . . they just aren't the guys for you. They are little league players, and you're in the major leagues."

At a stoplight, he leans his head against hers and says, "Will is a toad pretending to be a prince. You deserve better than that." She laughs through her tears and feels her heart lighten a little.

Once they arrive at her mom's house, the rain has stopped. He opens her car door for her and holds her in his arms, looking into her eyes, wiping away her tears. "A woman like you is a once-in-a-lifetime, Julie. Those guys will realize what they're missing, and they'll come crawling back. I want you to be the strong, beautiful, sexy woman you are and hold out for more. The right man could never take you for granted."

Nick gently kisses her forehead and holds her until the crying stops. "Do you feel any better?"

She sighs and dabs her eyes with a tissue. "My heart felt lost earlier . . . but it feels more at home now. Thank you, Nick."

He smiles at her. "The thing I love most about you, Julie, is that you live and love each day as if it's your last. You don't leave anything on the table, you never hold back. Don't ever change. One day a real man is going to hold you in his arms and never let you go."

She smiles. "I like the sound of that. Are you ready for some home cooking?"

Her family has started to gather out on her mom's front porch now. They've been anxiously awaiting her arrival and were looking forward to meeting Will. Instead, they get to spend the evening with Julie and Nick, the real man who showed up when she most needed him.

"It would be an honor to join you and your family for dinner, Julie." He smiles and waves at her family before getting her bags out of his truck and carrying them up the hill toward the house.

Cake in Bed

Julie's mom says, "Oh my gosh, what happened to Will? Is everything okay?" as they approach the porch. The entire family is standing outside concerned and waiting for answers. Julie looks at Nick and then looks back at her mom and bursts into tears. Her mom holds her while she tries to find the right words.

Nick jumps in and says, "Will had some . . . um . . . personal issues to attend to. He wasn't in the best state of mind to meet you so Julie told him to leave. She's had a really long day. She invited me instead, and I'm thrilled to get to see you again," he says, hugging everyone.

Her mom smiles and welcomes him inside. "It's nice for you to join us."

"Great to see you again, Judy. I hear you have a feast on the table." He hugs her mom and gives Julie a wink over her shoulder.

While he's greeting everyone, Julie's younger sister comes over to her and says, "You're way too important to let Will or any man get you down." She tears up and hugs her with all her might.

Julie's four-year-old nephew sees her crying at the dining room table and brings her his stuffed penguin and his blanket. He wraps it around her and hugs her, pats her head, and says, "Everything's going to be alright." Julie is overcome by his sweetness and hugs him tightly.

Within a few awkward minutes food is on the table, and Nick has the conversation flowing. Everyone is laughing and having fun, including Julie. She looks around at the happy faces of her family and then back at Nick and marvels at how personable he is. She feels loved and supported all around the table. It feels magical.

Her mom even gives Nick the honorary first serving of her well-loved homemade banana pudding for dessert. Nick beams with gratitude and keeps talking about how delicious everything is, even though Julie knows that he doesn't typically like bananas. Seeing his genuine appreciation makes her smile from a deep place within.

When they leave her mom's house hours later, no one even remembers that someone else was supposed to be there. Everyone was so happy to spend time with her and Nick.

After they share hugs and goodbyes, Nick carries their leftovers down to his truck and drives her home. It's late now, and she's so tired from the physically and emotionally exhausting day.

It's a dark and foggy night. Visibility is very low, taking them much longer to get back to her home in Malibu. She lies down in the front seat with her head on Nick's legs. "Is this okay?"

He looks down at the beautiful woman lying in his lap and smiles. He strokes her hair gently with his right hand as he drives with his left. She falls asleep.

When they arrive at her home, he lightly wakes her to lay her head on the seat as he gets out of the truck. He carries her things in and gently leads her inside. He waits in her kitchen while she changes into her pajamas and then tucks her into bed. "Nick . . . will you do something for me?" she asks, half-asleep.

Sitting on her bedside, gazing down at her, he replies, "Anything."

"Will you stay until I fall asleep?" she asks, twirling a piece of her hair.

"You got it." He kicks off his shoes and crawls into bed with her and allows her to rest her head on his chest. He kisses her forehead and holds her tightly. Within minutes, she falls asleep in his arms.

Nick gazes at her and gently strokes her hair as she sleeps. He studies her face and her breathing before shifting into a lying position, still holding her. He lies awake, eyes open, thinking, happy to be close with her, but not wanting her to be sad.

Reflecting on the day, he feels angry with Will for letting her down in such a big way. It took all he had to see Will sitting so smugly in that sports car and not say anything to him about his behavior. He didn't want to prolong the encounter or make it any more difficult for Julie.

He thinks about how he had such a surprisingly good time with her and her family tonight. It was so different from any family experience he's ever had. Being with Julie is easy, even when she's had a bad day.

He looks down at her head on his chest, gives a little smile, and closes his eyes to go to sleep.

Twenty-four

When Julie awakens the next morning, the sunbeams are already streaming in through the window.

She feels Nick's warm body spooning her from behind, his legs intertwined with hers. His arms are around her stomach and he shifts a little and cups his hand around her breast.

At first she's shocked and gets ready to roll over and push him away. Then, she realizes he's still asleep and completely unaware of what he's doing. And, as she lies there feeling his strong hand holding her breast, she actually likes the sensation.

Her heartbeat speeds up. She feels alive. She decides to close her eyes, relax, and enjoy the moment.

Nick is in a deep sleep and is making little noises. He starts gently kissing the back of her neck while pulling her closer to him. She gasps audibly. He may be asleep, but he's awakening new feelings within her.

Every cell in her body feels electric as his soft lips caress her neck and back. His warm breath leaves soft footprints as his tongue flickers against the tender skin along her hairline.

He squeezes her breast firmly but lovingly over her nightshirt, and she feels him hardening behind her. "Oh God, Julie," he whispers passionately.

She is getting swept away into the heat of the moment and doesn't know what to do. She wants to roll over and kiss him so badly. But she's afraid and doesn't want to lose his amazing friendship.

Luckily, she's the only one who's over thinking right now. Nick is asleep and dreaming and, from the sound of it, having a very good dream. She smiles knowing that it's a juicy dream about her.

He begins panting a little as he kisses her neck. "I want you. Let's make love," he whispers. She feels him gently thrust his pelvis into her backside.

As much as she's enjoying having a sneak peek into his hot, steamy dream, she starts to feel uncomfortable. What if she was the one dreaming out loud, and he let her get so deep into it? She would be mortified.

Reluctantly, she decides to pull away a bit without waking him. He reaches for her, but his hands can't find her anymore.

He's breathing heavily now. He starts to lightly rub his hand on himself over his clothes.

She can't believe how sexy he is. With every ounce of her being she wants to watch him, touch him, be so close with him, but she feels obligated to put a stop to it for his own good.

She snuggles back in with him, lying on her side facing him. He immediately holds her. "It's okay. We don't have to right now. I understand," he says and kisses her forehead still in a deep sleep.

Julie whispers, "Nick."

He responds, "I love you, Julie."

"I love you, too," she replies and decides to just rest with him until he wakes up.

An hour or so later, she awakens to an empty bed. Nick walks into her bedroom, still wearing his clothes from the day before. "Hi, beautiful. How'd you sleep?" he asks as he brings her a glass of water and sits on the side of the bed.

"I always sleep really well when you're nearby," she smiles as she drinks. "How about you?"

He takes a deep breath. "I have such intense dreams when I'm with you at night." She hands him the glass of water and he takes a drink. "I don't know what it is about being near you, but I sleep well and dream a lot more than usual."

With a sneaky smile, she asks, "What did you dream about last night?"

Nick takes a look in her big green eyes and for a moment, seems to consider telling her, but then looks away. "It's not important." He sighs. "What is important right now is making sure you're taken care of today."

"I'm okay, Nick," she says while she sits up in bed, her nightshirt clinging to her and revealing the soft angles of her body. "You were so amazing last night. Thank you for being you and for picking me up and for making everything wonderful with my family." She starts to tear up a little. "You're the best friend I've ever had."

He hugs her and says, "You're welcome. I'm so happy I could be there for you. And, I officially hate that guy. Please don't acquiesce to anything he asks again. He shouldn't even be allowed to speak your name after the way he behaved. You're much better off without him."

"And, thank you for staying with me last night. It could've been a hard night, but you made it so much better." He pulls away from her hug a bit and sits with his face close to hers, looking deep into her eyes. His blue eyes are piercing through her as he seems to be considering what to say next.

"What is it, Nick?" She feels slightly scared to ask.

"I don't want to upset you, Julie, but you're going to find out later anyway . . . I woke up about a half hour ago because your phone kept vibrating. I didn't want you to wake up, so I took it into the kitchen." Her heart is racing and she's afraid of what he's going to say next.

"Just know that everything is going to be okay." He pulls his phone from his pocket and shows it to her. Her stomach drops and the blood drains from her face as she sees what's on the screen. It's a paparazzi-style picture of her sobbing, a complete mess, on the loading dock outside of the Staples Center on *TMZ*. She swipes the photo and sees another, and another, and another of her sitting on her boxes, crumpled over with the horrid headline "Happily Never After: Literary Sweetheart Heartbroken."

"Oh my God!" she yells in disbelief. "Will! He must've taken pictures of me that day before he came over and introduced himself . . ." she trails off. "I can't believe it!" She's boiling and starts to get out of bed. Nick goes to hold her to keep her still. She struggles with him before relaxing. "I'm going to kill him!"

"It's okay, I know you want to kill him. And he deserves every bad thing that's coming to him," he affirms. "But you being in contact with him right now is only going to lead to more personal and professional pain." He continues to hold her tightly as she begins to release her tensed muscles and relax her body.

She starts to cry with big sobs. He feels her body shaking. "I'm here," he soothes her. "Everything's going to be okay. We'll get a good attorney and sue his ass as well as *TMZ* and *People*."

"Wait, why would we sue *People?*"

"Um, well . . ." he hesitates. "You're kinda on the cover of the magazine today, and probably not in the way you always envisioned."

"I hate him! How could he do this to me?"

Holding her still, he says, "He's a sleaze, Julie, it has nothing to do with you. That's probably why he broke things off abruptly last night. He knew these photos were going to come out today, and he couldn't face your family with his ill intentions."

"Oh my God! I don't know what to do, Nick. I hate feeling this way," she sobs into his shoulder.

He shifts positions and wipes her tears from her eyes. "You want me to go beat him up for you?" he asks in a Rocky Balboa accent. She laughs, surprising herself.

"What do you think I should do?" she asks with panic in her voice and pain in her eyes.

Nick thinks for a moment. "We should eat breakfast and strategize," he says as he stands up and pulls her hand to follow him into the kitchen. "You make yourself comfortable, I'll make breakfast while we brainstorm."

He puts on her girly red polka dot apron to make her smile. She sits on the kitchen counter near the stove. He starts making eggs.

"Okay, so we know that the photos are at least on *TMZ* and *People*, and possibly spreading like wildfire online," he says.

She sighs. "I'm so embarrassed," she says, cringing. He looks over at her and she makes a frowny face. He smiles.

"You're a writer, Julie—and a damn good one," he says. "You know . . . here's what you do. You could come up with a media-friendly backstory and pitch it to several of the talk shows. Then you could take the best offer, get paid for the TV appearance, and probably benefit a lot from the exposure. You may even get more fans from sharing a little piece of your heartbreak with them."

She looks at him with curiosity. "That's actually a really good idea. Who are you, and what did you do with my friend, Nick, the architect?" He laughs.

"You could lay low for twenty-four hours, talk with your attorney, and then come out with the 'full story' tomorrow. Chances are they'll be looking for you today and maybe all week, so make sure you look and feel amazing every time you leave your place . . . which won't be hard because you always look incredible."

He hands her a fork and a plate with sunny side up eggs just the way she likes them.

"And, if I were you, I wouldn't engage with Will at all. If anything, he'll be trying to bait you so he can sell your angry texts to the media," he says, leaning against the counter and eating his eggs.

"You're right. It's obviously all a game to him," she says dejectedly. "I just feel so used and embarrassed about the whole thing."

"This is going to be a blessing for you, Julie. I know it doesn't feel like it right now, but I know it will. You're a good person, and good things happen to good people. Somehow, in some way, this is going to benefit you."

"Thank you, Nick. I needed to hear that. And thank you for the yummy breakfast as well." She hops down off the counter and goes to wash her plate and grabs his empty plate on the way to the sink.

"I've got your back. We know the truth. That's what matters."

After breakfast, Julie goes back into her bedroom and flops down on the bed. "So, what do we do now?" she asks Nick. He turns the light off in the kitchen as he walks into the bedroom and flops down beside her.

"Is my life always going to be this tumultuous?" she ponders out loud and rolls onto her side to look at him.

He rolls toward her and props his head up on his arm. "I doubt it." He smiles. "It's just extra exciting right now while your career is taking off. I know you're going to continue to be a huge star and to shine so brightly and inspire millions of people, but it won't always have such fluctuations," he reassures her.

Her phone rings, interrupting their conversation. Nick grabs it from the dresser to hand it to her. Will's name comes across the screen. A feeling of panic seizes her stomach muscles. "May I?" he asks. Curious as to what he's going to do, she nods.

He answers the phone and puts it on speaker but doesn't say a word. "Hello? Julie?" Will says. He motions to her to stay quiet. She freezes at the sound of Will's voice and feels sick, like she might puke any moment.

"Look, Julie, I'm sorry about the pictures but a man's gotta do what a man's gotta do. Business has been slow and I gotta eat. Just wanted to tell you that you didn't deserve what happened yesterday," he says with bravado. "Are you there?" he asks, sounding annoyed.

"Well, for whatever it's worth, you're amazing on every level. See ya around." Nick hangs up the phone and sets it back on the dresser.

"Told you he's a douche . . . how are you feeling?"

"Confused. I would never do that to anyone . . . dump someone right before meeting their family, after having wild sex with them the night before, and then sell photos of them in their most vulnerable behind-the-scenes moments. He's disgusting."

Her phone rings again. Nick grabs it, and it's her publisher. He hands the phone to her. "Should I take it?" she asks frantically. He nods.

She sits up in bed. "Hello?" she answers, feeling nervous about the conversation that's about to unfold.

"Yes, I saw a few of the pictures and the headlines." Nick sits down next to her on the bed and rubs her leg comfortingly.

"What? Really?" She sounds shocked. She stands up and starts walking around the room while she listens.

"Tomorrow? Yes, I can be on a plane tomorrow." She looks at Nick and he listens intently. "I'll need an extra ticket to bring my security with me."

"Okay, see you then." She hangs up the phone and slowly sits on the bed.

She sits there in silence, stunned. "What happened? Tell me!" Nick says.

"You aren't going to believe this," she says. "Apparently there's been a huge outpouring of support for me online, and the book orders have been coming in like crazy all morning. We're about to go into a second printing! My publisher wants me to make an appearance on a few morning talk shows in New York to thank my fans and then take me to dinner to discuss a new, more lucrative contract for my next book! They're flying me first class tomorrow! Suddenly I'm some kind of accidental rock star."

Nick stands up. "I knew it! I knew something good would come from this!" He laughs and lifts her off the bed in a big hug and twirls her around. "That's wonderful!"

"And, you can come with me if you'd like. They're giving me an extra ticket for my security." She grins as she catches her breath. "Please come to New York with me. We'll have fun, and I'll even buy you a hot dog!" she says playfully.

"I would love to join you. Let me see what I can do with my schedule. Nothing is as important to me as your security and your happiness right now. You're a rising star and I'm honored to get to be on the journey with you."

Julie dances around with him before he pulls her down onto the bed with him. They both laugh. "You know, I treasure these times with you," he says tenderly, pulling her hair away from her eyes. "You're such an amazing woman."

She looks at him and smiles. "And you're an amazing man. I'm so happy right now!"

"All of your dreams are coming true!"

Twenty-five

Julie hears Nick's special knock on her door as he peeks around the corner. "Good morning, gorgeous! Are you ready for a Big Apple adventure?"

He comes in and scoops her up in his arms with a big hug. She laughs. "Yes!" She can't help but notice that he looks so handsome in his dress shirt, nice pants, and leather shoes.

"Let me carry that for you," Nick says as he sees her struggling in her miniskirt with her oversized suitcase. "Are you sure you got everything you need in here?" he teases her. They both laugh.

At the airport, she starts to relax and have fun, walking around and joking with Nick. After buying some snacks and a bottle of water in the little airport shop, a girl approaches her. "You're Julie, right?" Julie smiles and nods. "Oh my God! I'm a big fan and I just want you to know that you're awesome!" She gives her a hug and asks if she can take a selfie with her. Julie says okay and secretly feels grateful that she took the time to put makeup on that morning.

As the girl walks away, Nick looks down at Julie with admiration. "You know, you're really something special to make that girl's day like that." They smile at each other.

Cake in Bed

When they get on the plane, she's excited to sit in first class. Nick gives her the window seat, her favorite. As the other passengers walk past their seats to board, she hears whispering and starts to feel a little self-conscious. Nick notices her discomfort and pulls a hoodie out of his carry-on bag. "Here, you can put the hood over your eyes and relax with your music," he says, handing it to her.

"You're amazing, Nick! Thank you." She puts his sweater on and smells the intoxicating scent of him. She goes to pull her earphones from her bag only to discover that she's forgotten them at home.

He takes his earphones off and hands them to her. "I wasn't really listening to anything anyway." He smiles.

She puts his earphones on, pulls the soft gray hood down over her eyes, and leans against the window. He looks over at her, this tiny and powerful woman who's growing into the mogul that he always knew she would be. At the same time, she's his best friend, with a beautiful, sometimes fragile heart, and the person he adores most. He closes his eyes in gratitude to be here to protect her and guard her heart.

He's startled to feel her warm hand reach for his. He looks over at her, still curled up in the window, but wanting to feel connected to him. He holds her hand and caresses her skin gently with his thumb.

They're both awakened by the flight attendant as she's preparing the cabin for landing. Julie can hardly believe that she's slept through the entire flight. "Wow! I never sleep on planes!" she says to Nick. Still a little groggy, he looks over at her and smiles with sleepy eyes.

He helps her with her bags as they exit the plane and come through baggage claim. "There's supposed to be a driver waiting for us outside these doors," she says while looking around.

But as they walk through the exit doors, they both get a big surprise. There's a crowd of people waiting there and at first, Julie doesn't think anything of it. But in a flash, people are approaching her and taking pictures of her without asking. A few bold people are even touching her shoulders and grabbing her hands. She feels instantly overwhelmed and tries to back away from the crowd. They follow her movements, as everyone seems to want to get a piece of her or a picture of her.

Nick is shocked and appalled by the presumptive behavior of the crowd. He puts his body between her and the people in an effort to shield her. "Whoa! Clear the path!" he says forcefully. "Stop touching her. Show some respect. Give her space!"

She holds onto the back of his shirt with both hands, ducking her head and tucking her face against his back as the crowd around them grows. She can't even see where they're going, but trusts Nick to guide her while she hides her face. He keeps moving forward, carrying their bags and quickly searching for their driver.

Julie feels frightened and keeps her head down, following Nick until he guides her into the back of a black car. He quickly gets her into the back seat, closes the car door, and then makes sure the driver puts their bags into the trunk. He jumps into the car with her and asks the driver to lock the doors. She hears the click of the lock just as people are approaching the car and banging on the windows.

He asks the driver to put the privacy screen up and he complies. Julie curls up in fetal position in the corner of the back seat of the limo.

Nick goes right to her and holds her, one arm around her back and the other around her knees, her head on his shoulder. "What was that?! That was so scary," she whispers to him.

"That was crazy!" he agrees. "Thank God you weren't alone."

Her body begins to shake. "Maybe this wasn't such a good idea."

"I know it was overwhelming, Julie, but these people love you. It doesn't justify them touching you and taking pictures without your permission. I really hate that! But, if you could hear what they were saying, they are in support of you."

She looks up at him with tears in her eyes. "Really?" She feels her cheeks burning and her throat tighten up.

"Yes, these are fans of yours who want to be near you, to experience the magic of you. And, maybe they need some supervision, but they want to show their support for you. Congratulations, you're officially a celebrity." He laughs.

"I don't know about this. I don't like people grabbing me and blocking our path. And I hate paparazzi-style pictures." She gives a heavy sigh as the tears stop.

"I understand. I don't like that either, but no one will ever block your path when you're with me," he reassures her.

The car stops in front of the hotel. He pulls his hoodie up over her head and covers her eyes. "Hold my hand and we'll get you inside. Don't worry, I'll keep you safe."

As the driver opens the door, Nick steps out first and then offers his hand to help her onto the sidewalk. The driver delivers their suitcases to the bellhop and takes them inside the hotel. He comes over to her and says, "Julie! I just want you to know that I felt bad about those pictures and that I'm cheering you on!"

She smiles and says, "Thank you."

Nick sees the crowd starting to gather around them and quickly leads her into the hotel lobby. "I'll get us checked in," he says. As they approach the desk, the hotel staff is happy to see her and everyone is friendly.

Still feeling cautious, she keeps the hood up to cover the evidence from her crying in the car. Nick sees the hotel staff's excitement and curiosity and asks them to give her some privacy right now. They oblige.

He leads her into the elevator and asks the rest of the crowd if they can be alone. The staff and hotel guests stand quietly outside the elevator as the doors close. He turns to face her, slowly pulls back the hoodie from her eyes, and removes it from her head.

She looks up at him and takes a deep breath. "Do I look horror film worthy?" she laughs a little.

"Never," he says with authority and a smile.

When the elevator door opens, they're in the foyer of a very fancy room. "Wow," she says as he uses the key to open the beautiful door. "They gave you the penthouse, Julie!" he says with joy. "You're a really big deal!"

He opens the door to the most breathtaking hotel room that Julie's ever seen. It has a wide view of the city skyline, three fireplaces, a claw-foot bathtub, a dining room, a sitting room, and a gorgeous bed.

"I think this is the most beautiful place I've ever been!" she says in disbelief.

There's a vibrant flower arrangement on the table along with chilled champagne, chocolate-covered strawberries, and a note from her publisher congratulating her.

"Wow!"

The doorbell rings and in walks a bellhop, a handsome blond twenty-something, with their bags. Nick ushers him in and tips him for his help. Before he leaves, he walks over to Julie and introduces himself.

"Hi, Miss Julie, I'm Sven. I'll be your butler for this week while you're staying with us. If there's anything you need, and I do mean anything at all, food, wine, bubbles, a hot date, please press 3 on your phone and I'll come running." He winks at her and Nick escorts him out the door.

"And now you have your own butler!" He laughs.

"Was he hitting on me?" she asks honestly.

"Um, yes. Without a doubt."

"Weird."

"Better get used to it. You're a hot, single, sexy, and successful woman. Everyone is going to want to go out with you."

"But I'm a mess right now," she protests. "My makeup is all over my face, my hair is frizzy from the hoodie, and I'm wearing a man's sweater that is at least four sizes too big."

Nick walks over to her and gently takes his sweater off of her as if he's taking her coat. She stands there in her denim miniskirt, black t-shirt, patterned tights, and black knee boots. "It's like I've been telling you, Julie, you're a super-sexy woman. None of that other stuff really matters." He hangs his sweater in the closet. "Not to anyone of substance anyway."

He walks over to the table where she's sniffing the flowers. "All of those things you listed are just the icing and sprinkles on the cake. *You* are the cake. And only a man who realizes that is worthy of you."

"Thank you, Nick. You always know what to say to make me feel better." She picks up a chocolate-covered strawberry and offers it to him. He opens his mouth playfully, and she teases him with it for a moment before allowing him to bite it. They both laugh.

"How about some champagne?" he asks.

"I would love some," she says as she unzips her boots and kicks them off into the floor.

He pours two flutes of champagne and walks around the massive penthouse suite to find her. He hears a Katy Perry song pouring from the bedroom and knows she must be there. He comes around the corner into the bedroom to find her jumping on the giant bed and giggling. He smiles at the scene unfolding before him.

He carefully sets the champagne flutes down on the nightstand and kicks off his shoes. "May I join you?" he asks charmingly.

"You better!" She laughs. They jump on the gigantic bed together while the music blares.

He grabs her hands and jumps facing her, watching her hair bounce up and down on her shoulders and twirling her around like they're dancing in the air.

Nick accidentally steps on a pillow, throws off his balance, and lands on the bed on his butt. Julie stops jumping immediately and drops to her knees in front of him. "Are you okay?" He's cracking up laughing, and as soon as she knows he's all right, she laughs too.

He reaches for the glasses and hands her one. He raises his flute into the air towards her. "A toast to you, Julie," he says, "and the magic you're creating in the world. To letting go of what doesn't fit so you can welcome all that you truly deserve." He smiles and clinks her glass. They both take a sip.

She raises her glass to him. "To you, your freedom, and your future business. May all of your wildest dreams come true . . . no one deserves it more than you!" They clink glasses and drink again.

"So I was thinking that it could be a little crazy taking you out to dinner this evening now that people know where you're staying." Her face gets serious again. "How about I treat you to an amazing room-service dinner here in this palace?"

"That sounds perfect, Nick! Tomorrow will be a full day with TV appearances, meetings, and dinner with my publisher. Let's leave the craziness for tomorrow and just relax tonight."

Twenty-six

Julie stands by the panoramic windows looking out at the view of the sunset behind the city skyline. She sips from her champagne flute and ponders the meaning of it all. *This has been a crazy week,* she thinks.

She recalls the wild night of passion she had with Will. She was floating on cloud nine before he dropped a series of bombs on their relationship the next day. Thinking back, she remembers him pressuring her to go further and further that night, to the point where she was uncomfortable with what was happening, but trying to be open-minded and loving. She didn't like the way that felt or the way he treated her the day they were supposed to see her family.

Looking out onto the city, she remembers the way Nick rescued her from that awkward situation and made everything okay again with her family. She thinks about discovering that Will had taken and sold photos of her to the media, and how disgraced and humiliated she felt in front of millions of people as a result.

In her mind she replays her publisher's phone call from yesterday. She can't believe that in the last 24 hours, she's learned that her book is going gangbusters and that they're flying her to New York for a bunch of cool appearances and to ultimately give her more money. She smiles at how often blessings come in disguise in her life.

Taking another sip, she thinks about the unexpected crowd that had surrounded her at the airport. *I really thought they might get out of control and hurt me. But, I felt safer knowing that Nick was there to protect me. I always feel better when he's around.*

She recalls the joyful look on his face when he came through the bedroom door and saw her jumping on the bed, and the way he happily joined in. She smiles.

Nick walks over and stands next to her at the window, admiring the view. "Okay, I talked with our friend Sven and ordered us a mouth-watering, mostly healthy three-course celebration meal. It'll be here in an hour or so."

She turns to him and smiles. "That's perfect. Just enough time to get in a quick and dirty workout," she says, walking toward her suitcase.

"Where are you going to work out?"

"I was thinking about the hotel gym."

"Um, I don't know if you're going to be able to do that today. You know, with the way people are following you," he says apologetically. "What if we run the stairs together? This is a really tall building, and no one will be looking for you on the stairs."

"Great idea! Let's run stairs." She pulls her workout clothes from her suitcase and goes into the palatial bathroom to change.

She comes out wearing one of her cute little workout skirts and a tight-fitting tank. Nick can't help but check her out while she's leaning over putting on her tennis shoes. He quickly looks away and goes to change into his workout wear. "Ready?"

"That was the best workout I've had all week!" Julie says, panting, as Nick opens the penthouse door for her. "It was a good one!" he agrees.

"Twenty minutes until dinner arrives . . . I'm going to take a quick shower," she says, walking to the bathroom.

Running stairs with Nick was actually fun. And, he was right, no one takes the stairs and no one saw them there. *This trip is a lot more fun with him.*

While she's showering, Nick takes off his sweaty shirt and stands by the window overlooking the city at night. He's gulping water and remembering how sexy Julie looked running those stairs in that little skirt. *What's happening to me? I'm crazy about that woman.*

She comes out of the bathroom ten minutes later, hair combed but wet with a fluffy bath towel wrapped around her. She sees him staring out the window deep in thought from across the room. The muscles in his back ripple as he takes a swig of water. He turns around and they both gasp when they see each other.

Her face turns red and she quickly goes through her suitcase to find something comfortable to wear. He clears his throat, looks away, and walks into the bathroom to get cleaned up for dinner.

When he emerges from the bathroom freshly showered and shaved in a t-shirt and jeans, he finds her lying on the couch responding to messages wearing, a satin animal print pajama set. *God, she's always smoking hot.*

"Our butler just called, dinner will be here any minute," she says happily.

Just then the doorbell rings. "I'll get it," Nick says. "You have perfect timing, my friend," he tells Sven as he rolls his fancy cart into the room.

"Where would you like to dine this evening?" asks Sven.

"Maybe near the window . . . what do you prefer, Julie?" asks Nick.

"Near the window sounds great." She turns her phone off and joins them by the window.

Sven looks her up and down. "Nice pajamas."

Embarrassed, Julie forgot that she was wearing no makeup and pajamas and gives a timid "Thank you."

Sven sets the cart up as a table, lights a candle, turns on the fireplace, and brings chairs over for them. Once they're seated, he pours them some fresh champagne and lifts the food cover to reveal two bowls of lobster bisque and an enormous platter of halibut served with spinach. "I'll put dessert in the refrigerator for you. *Bon appétit*," he says as he leaves.

"This looks amazing, Nick!" she says excitedly.

"Good, because you deserve amazing! And, by the way, you look absolutely stunning."

"You are always so sweet to me. Thank you, Nick."

Nick smiles at her and looks serious for a moment. She can tell he's deep in thought about something important to him.

"What are you thinking about?" she asks curiously while slurping a little lobster bisque from her spoon.

"I wanted to share something with you. Something that I've been thinking about a lot lately." She looks happily at him and patiently waits to hear more.

He takes a sip of his soup, swallows it, and says, "I've been doing a lot of reflecting on my life lately. When I sold my business, you were the only person who fully supported me doing that. Everyone else seemed to think I'd gone crazy on some level, even Asa." He pauses. "Maybe I have."

She simply smiles at him while enjoying her soup and looking into his contemplative blue eyes.

"It means a lot that you believe in me, Julie. More than you know."

He takes another spoonful of soup into his mouth. "As you may remember, growing the business I acquired has been something of an obsession of mine for the past few years. I wanted to prove to myself and to everyone I could do it, that I could be successful."

He dabs his mouth with his napkin and drinks from his water glass.

"Now that I've accomplished that goal, it doesn't seem as important to me. Don't get me wrong, I love my work, but I feel like there was always something missing that I can't quite put my finger on.

"I never really saw myself as more than a business owner. Probably because I've been so focused on that role. I'm not sure what my next move is, but I'm grateful that you believe in me. Thank you for standing by me and supporting my dreams." He smiles and offers her some halibut.

"I'm so proud of you, Nick. You wanted to grow a business, you worked hard, and you were wildly successful at it. You also recognized when it was no longer fulfilling to you and took an opportunity to make a change. It's not easy to follow your heart, but you did it! And I know that whatever you do next will be extraordinary because that's who you are."

They both look up from their dinners and smile at each other.

Nick says thoughtfully, "I think I need more balance in my life. Being here with you is showing me that there's more to life than closing deals and building things. You open my eyes and inspire me to be more than I thought possible in the past."

She reaches for his hand across the table. "That's awesome, Nick, because you do the same for me!" She gives his hand a quick squeeze and goes back to cutting her halibut.

"Plus, you need a bodyguard and I'm happy to help," he laughs.

A few minutes later he asks, "Do you ever miss your ex-husband?"

She looks up at him mid-bite with surprise. She thinks for a moment. "Surprisingly, not really." She smiles at the realization. She hasn't thought about it in months. "Is that bad? Why do you ask?"

"I was just wondering because I haven't missed Allison at all since we broke up. I was feeling a little guilty that I didn't have those feelings. I feel better now knowing that you're in the same boat." He smiles and finishes the last bite on his plate.

She sets her fork down. "That is interesting. What do you think it means?"

"I'm not sure, but I think that it's a sign that we did the right thing by not spending our lives with people that we could go days and weeks without even thinking about."

"I agree," she responds thoughtfully. "Sometimes I miss the idea of the person he represented, just like with Evan and Will. But if I'm really honest with myself, I don't actually miss them. It's more like missing a soul mate or a partner that I wanted, but never really had."

He looks at her intensely, as if studying her while deep in thought. "That makes sense."

She changes the subject. "I'm so happy that we decided to stay in tonight. Thank you for the great dinner, Nick!"

He smiles and says, "Wait until you see dessert!"

"Oh my goodness! I'm not sure if I should have any . . . you know I'm going to be on all those shows tomorrow. I feel a little self-conscious," she says sheepishly.

Nick looks serious again. "Julie, your body is incredibly beautiful. I love your feminine curves and your shape. That being said, I totally respect your decision to enjoy dessert or pass, I just want you to know that you'll look amazing tomorrow regardless."

"Thanks, Nick. I think I'll save dessert for tomorrow night and go take a bath in that gorgeous tub." She finishes her dinner and places her napkin from her lap onto her plate. "Dinner was perfect," she says as she stands.

He reaches for her hand and says, "You are perfect," then kisses her hand lightly. "Enjoy your bath."

Twenty-seven

Nick curls up on the couch in the living room to relax while Julie soaks in her bubble bath. He feels like the luckiest man on Earth to get to share this hotel suite and these moments with her. As he reflects, the champagne starts getting to him and he gives in to his sleepiness and dozes despite his best efforts to stay awake.

When Julie emerges from the bathroom, she sees the bed turned down for her with a chocolate mint on the pillow. *I love this hotel.* She looks around for Nick and is surprised to find him sleeping on the sofa.

She thinks for a moment if maybe he intended to sleep there instead of in the bed with her. There was only one bed, and maybe he thought it would be presumptuous for him to assume he would be in it. She's tempted to just go to bed, but knows that she won't sleep as well wondering about him all night.

She leans down and whispers in his ear, "Nick."

He doesn't move at all. She touches his shoulder and whispers once again, a little louder, "Nick." Still no reaction.

This time she touches his chest, putting her palm on his heart and whispers, "Hey, handsome." He stirs and slowly opens his eyes. "Hey you. How was your bath?" He sits up as she stands.

"It was wonderful and relaxing. I'm so sleepy now."

"I know what you mean. I sat down for a minute and fell asleep!"

They both smile.

"You have a big day tomorrow. So exciting!" he says, trying to keep his eyes open.

"Yes, thanks for the lovely evening. It was amazing."

He smiles.

"You know what would make it even more amazing?" she asks playfully, feeling bold but scared.

"What?" he asks.

"If you would come to bed now so we can get a good night's sleep," she says with a sneaky smile.

He laughs and stands up, hugs her and kisses her on the forehead. "I didn't want to assume. It's okay with me to sleep here if you'd prefer me to. I respect you and I'm happy to do whatever's best for you."

"Really?"

"Really."

"Tell me the truth . . . where do you prefer to sleep?" she asks, looking into his eyes.

"Well, if I could, I would sleep as close as I could to you every night."

She smiles and grabs his hand. "Let's go to bed, Nick."

He holds her hand and happily follows her into the bedroom. They curl up together in the beautiful bed, him spooning her and holding her tight. "Goodnight, Jules," he says as he falls asleep behind her.

"Sweet dreams," she mumbles, happily drifting off to sleep.

"Good morning! Are you excited?" Nick asks as Julie wakes up beside him. He's been awake for an hour, quietly doing some research on his phone.

She looks over at him, smiles sleepily, and sits up in bed. "Wow . . . I had the most magnificent dream! I'll tell you tonight."

"Can't wait," he says with a smile. "What can I do to help you this morning?"

She thinks for a moment. "Well, I need to get showered, get dressed, eat breakfast, do my hair and makeup, and figure out the order of the appearances. My publisher has a driver arranged to take us from place to place. Are you sure you want to spend the day traipsing around the city with me and the media?"

"Are you kidding? I'm excited for you and want to be there with you. Someone's gotta protect you and get the good shots!"

"I'm glad you're coming." She smiles. "You make everything more fun."

"Okay, I'll order us some breakfast and shower after you," he says picking up the hotel phone. "I'll brief you on the shows while you're getting ready. I've been doing a little research this morning."

"You're amazing, Nick!" She leans over and kisses him on the cheek before getting out of bed to get a shower.

He hears the water start to run. She pokes her head out through the crack in the bathroom door. "You're brilliant . . . Thank you!"

Twenty-eight

Nick and Julie get back to their room and she immediately flops down on the sofa. "I'm so exhausted! I think I had too much champagne . . . way too much champagne."

"You had a huge day and have been going nonstop since early this morning," he says taking off his shoes. "What an amazing day . . . so much to celebrate!"

She smiles but can barely keep her eyes open. "My body is so tired and sore from being in heels all day . . . I don't think I can move another inch."

He hands her a bottle of water. "Well, I guess you're just going to have to sleep on the couch in your fancy dress then," he teases her.

Eyes closed, she takes a sip and then smiles at him. "Can you please take me to bed?"

Nick pauses for a moment, thinking about how much he's wanted to hear those words come out of her mouth. He walks over to her and scoops her up off of the sofa, one arm around her back and the other supporting her legs. He easily lifts her and carries her into the bedroom. Her body hangs limp in his strong arms. She's already falling asleep.

He lays her gently on the bottom of the bed while he gets the covers and pillows ready at the top. He leaves the lights off but can see her clearly by the light of moon from the window.

"Mmm," she groans in frustration as she tries unsuccessfully to reach the zipper on the back of her dress. She squirms a little until Nick puts his hand on her hip.

"Relax for a moment, Julie, and I'll help you."

He carefully undoes the straps on her shoes, pulls them off, and places them on the floor away from the bed. She wiggles, fighting through drowsiness to get under the covers. He gently takes off her earrings, her necklace, and her bracelet and places them on the nightstand. His fingers find the zipper pull on her back and he slowly unzips her dress, revealing her bare back underneath.

She quickly shimmies out of her dress and lies on top of the covers in nothing but her red lace thong panties. He can see the roundness of her bare breasts by the light of the moon.

Oh my God, she's even more gorgeous naked. He's instantly turned on and tries to look away. She's a little drunk and tired, and he doesn't want to take advantage of her.

He tries to hand her his shirt to put on, but she pushes it away. She just wants to get under the covers and to finally get to sleep. He lifts her up and tucks her in the covers. He's surprised when she starts pulling at his shirt, trying to take it off. He assists in removing it and then tries to keep his distance in the king-size bed. He keeps his pants on.

"Where are you?" Julie whispers.

"I'm over here," he says and offers her his hand from across the bed. "Are you going to sleep like that?" he asks as he feels his heart pounding in his chest.

"I always sleep naked when I'm alone at home," she says matter-of-factly.

Nick is so turned on he keeps to his side of the bed and tries to distract himself. "Goodnight, Julie. I'm really proud of you," he says as he rolls away from her. It's so difficult to turn his back toward her, but he wants to respect her space.

All he can think about is how perfect her body is and what it would feel like to touch her, to give her so much pleasure. He's surprised when she curls up behind him, her arms around his stomach, and her firm nipples pressed against his back. The feeling of her flesh against his takes him over the top.

Despite his best efforts, his body is reacting, and he can't think clearly. Her hand starts rubbing his chest and abs, and slowly starts moving down his body seductively. He imagines her touching him in his most forbidden zone, the way he has many times before. But not like this. *Oh God.* He quickly gets up out of bed and goes into the bathroom.

Julie awakens late in the morning. She's alone, almost naked, and shivering from the chill. She lies in bed for a few minutes wondering what happened the night before after the big celebration dinner with her publisher. She gathers the sheet around her as best she can and goes out into the suite to find Nick. She sees him resting on the sofa under a blanket.

When she walks into the room, he sits up, wraps the blanket around his bare shoulders, and walks over to greet her. Her hair is wild, and she still has most of her makeup on from the night before.

"Good morning, Julie," he says as he wraps his arms and blanket around her. *She looks sexy as hell wrapped up in that sheet,* he thinks.

"What happened last night? Are you upset with me, Nick?" she asks quietly. He can tell that she's confused and disappointed that he didn't stay with her.

"Not at all." He kisses her on the forehead, grabs her hand, and leads her to sit on the couch with him. "I'm upset with myself about last night."

She shivers and he instinctively puts his blanket fully around her, wrapping her up, and exposing his upper body. "Why?" she asks. He goes over to the closet and puts on a t-shirt and his hoodie before sitting back on the sofa with her.

"You are an extremely sexy woman, Julie. The sexiest woman I've ever seen." He looks into her big green eyes and takes a deep breath. "It was hard for me to resist you last night."

She feels confused. "What do you mean? Why would you want to sleep away from me?"

"I had a little too much champagne last night . . . I think maybe we both did. When you took off your dress, you were almost naked. I tried not to look, but I definitely peeked . . . a few times." He sounds upset with himself.

"Then, I tried to keep to one side of the bed. It was so hard not being close to you. When you rolled over to me and I could feel your nakedness against my skin, I had to get up," he says apologetically. He puts his hand on her leg. "I'm sorry I wasn't strong enough to walk away sooner. I hope you understand."

She just looks at him while thinking, trying to figure him out.

He squeezes her leg. "How are you feeling?"

"Umm . . . kinda embarrassed," she admits. "I didn't mean to put you in an awkward position. I'm sorry."

He lunges over to hold her. "I understand how you could feel that way, but you have nothing to be embarrassed or sorry about. I had a great time with you last night. You didn't do anything wrong. I just need to make sure that I'm always respectful of you and our relationship."

She hugs him. He looks into her eyes. "I have this overwhelming urge to protect you, even if that means it's from me. It was hard coming in here knowing that you were in the bedroom. I never want to disappoint you . . . it was the only way I could resist you last night. I'm sorry."

"Oh Nick, you're such a wonderful man and an incredible friend. I get it. Thank you for being a class act."

She playfully pulls his hoodie up over his head and asks, "What adventures shall we have on our last day in New York?"

He smiles. "How about we start with some breakfast?"

"Great idea! Do you want your usual? I'll call Sven," she chirps as she reaches for the phone.

"Perfect, thank you! What shall we do while we wait?" he asks her.

"Hmm . . ." She pretends to consider the possibilities. "I missed you last night. Why don't we cuddle?" she gives him a sneaky smile.

He lies down on the sofa and opens his arms to her with a smile. She adjusts the sheet and blanket making sure that's she fully wrapped up like a burrito. They both laugh.

She lies down beside him and nestles her head under his chin, against his chest. He wraps his arms around her and they both relax.

When the doorbell rings, they are both so comfortable that neither of them want to move. Nick gets up and answers the door. Julie sits on the sofa wrapped in her bedding.

Sven comes in, sets their breakfast plates on the coffee table near her and then gathers his cart by the door. Nick walks him out to give him a tip and asks him to bring some roses to surprise Julie later that day.

While they're outside the door, Sven says, "I gotta give you a high five, man."

Confused, Nick high-fives him back and asks why.

"Are you hittin' that, bro?"

He starts feeling himself heat up a bit and stays calm. "What are you talking about?"

"That ass, man . . . that sexy, sexy ass." Sven laughs. "You're a lucky man!"

"Look, Sven"—he takes a deep breath and says sternly, "She's a classy, sophisticated woman. Not just some 'sexy ass' that you can go around objectifying. Don't ever talk about her like that again." He turns away from Sven to go back into the room. "Please have the roses here by 5 tonight. Thank you." He goes back into the room where Julie is already eating her breakfast.

"Everything okay?" she asks while enjoying her omelet.

"Everything's perfect." He joins her on the sofa and chows down on his meal.

Twenty-nine

"Thank you for a magical time in New York, Nick," Julie says as they land in Los Angeles.

"Thank *you* for a magical time in New York," he says to her with a smile. "Are you excited about your birthday this weekend?"

"Oh, we've had so much excitement, I almost forgot! I wonder what you have up your sleeve?" she says playfully.

He winks at her. "Don't worry, you'll love it."

"Hey birthday girl! How are you today?" asks Nick as he walks through Julie's front door.

"Hey you! It's a great day that's just getting started. I slept in a little bit." She walks over and gives him a huge hug.

"Wonderful! I'm on my way home from the gym. You ready for your spa day?"

"I'm so excited! It was incredibly thoughtful of you to give me a relaxing massage for my birthday!"

"Awesome. We're still on for tonight, right?" he asks.

"Yes, no hot dates lined up yet," she teases. "Remind me what we're doing again."

He chuckles. "Nice try. I don't want to spoil your birthday surprise. I'll pick you up from the spa at 6?"

"See you then!"

Julie arrives at the spa and immediately feels more relaxed. It's like an oasis for the senses. As she walks through the carved oak doors, she feels the cool air on her skin and smells the luscious scent of orange blossom. She goes to the front desk to check in and upon arrival, is given a beautiful flower arrangement with a card from Nick.

"Oh wow! What an incredible surprise!"

The sleek and sophisticated spa woman behind the desk coolly says, "Mr. Bliss wanted to make sure you feel extra special today."

"Mission accomplished!" Julie responds.

"The day has just begun," the woman says while giving her a tour of the spa. "Your day includes any fitness class you'd like to attend, a spa lunch, a ninety-minute massage, use of the pool, Jacuzzi, sauna, and hair and makeup appointments this afternoon."

Julie enjoys a dream day at the spa, taking an aerial yoga class, getting a hot stone massage, eating a delicious and healthy lunch, relaxing on a float in the private pool, and showering before her hair and makeup appointment.

While at her appointment, the stylist asks her what she's going to wear. "I don't know actually, Kelly," she says.

"Why don't you wear this?" Kelly pulls a beautiful purple dress from behind the door.

"It's so breathtaking!" says Julie.

"Yes, Mr. Bliss brought it for you to wear this evening."

"Really?!" She feels so excited to have such a luxurious day and then get to wear a gorgeous new dress that was handpicked for her by someone she loves very much. "This is a dream-come-true day!"

Kelly smiles and continues to work her magic. When she turns the chair around for her to see the final result, Julie is speechless. "Oh my God! I hardly recognize myself. You did an amazing job!" She starts to tear up.

"Don't cry, you'll ruin your makeup!" laughs Kelly while handing her a tissue. "I'm glad you're happy. Now let's get you into your dress."

When Julie comes out of the bathroom in the purple dress, everyone's jaws drop. "You look absolutely stunning," says Kelly.

"I actually feel stunning thanks to your hair and makeup. Can't wait to see what Nick has planned for tonight! This is already my best birthday ever."

"Your husband is so romantic."

Julie smiles. "He's just my best friend."

"Swoon!" says Kelly with a wink.

When Julie walks into the spa lobby, Nick is there waiting in a handsome blue suit. She sees him from afar standing at the desk. The stylish and sophisticated spa woman is doing her best to flirt with him, but he's not taking the bait. Julie smiles.

He turns around just in time to see Julie walk down the hallway toward him. His mouth gapes open a little and his eyes sparkle.

"Wow. Simply wow," he says as he hugs her and kisses her on the cheek. "You look even more stunning than usual, and I didn't think that was possible."

"Thank you for the beautiful flowers, pampering day, and amazing dress, Nick. I feel like a princess!"

"It's my absolute pleasure. You deserve it all." He kisses her cheek, puts his arm out for her to grab, and escorts her to his truck.

"You're so mysterious. Where are we going?" she asks playfully as he starts the truck.

He looks over at her and runs his hand through his hair. "Let's run by your place first so we can drop off the flowers and pick up your jacket in case it gets cool tonight." He motions to the arrangement in her lap. "I picked the lilacs and roses because I know those are your favorites."

"I love them. Everything today has been perfect. Thank you!" She's so happy that she can't help but have a permanent smile on her face.

When they arrive at her new home, Nick helps her out of the truck and carries the bouquet for her. As she unlocks her front door, she's startled to hear "Surprise!" and to see friends from all over the world in her foyer.

"Oh my God!" she squeals as she's inundated with hugs, kisses, and love from her favorite people. Tears flow from her eyes as she looks around the room at the faces of her friends, some of whom she hasn't seen in person in years.

She turns around and looks at Nick. He looks back at her with love. "You—how did you do this?" she stammers out. "You're simply amazing. I don't know how you pulled this off, but I'm so grateful." She kisses him on the cheek and turns back to face her friends.

Music starts to play in the background as the room fills with clinking glasses, delicious appetizers, and buzzing conversation.

Local friends August, Jolene, Stephanie, and Winston are there to toast and celebrate her birthday. Her friend Sandra is there from Boston, Ranj from Canada, and Priyanka all the way from London. The doorbell rings and Julie is delighted when Rebecca, Jackie, Angie, and Eve join the celebration.

Looking around her dining room she sees balloons and festive party decorations.

"Picture with the birthday girl?" her friend Ben asks. She obliges, and they have fun posing and making silly faces.

Nick comes over and asks if she's hungry. "Absolutely," she says with a smile.

"Great, let's sit at the table and dinner will be served."

Julie sits between Nick and her friend Patrick. Everyone is anxious to hear about Julie's new publishing contract, her home, and her special spa day. As they talk and catch up, a waiter comes and serves them gourmet mini deep-dish pizzas with choose-your-own toppings. Julie laughs with delight when she sees the food. "You know me so well, Nick!"

He laughs. He feels full of joy to give her the gift of a perfect birthday, something that he knows she's never had.

She's excited to hear what everyone's been up to and spend time with each of her special friends. Champagne and laughter flows throughout the room. Then, the waiter dims the lights and brings out the cake, a beautiful lemon cake confection with buttercream icing. He places it in front of Julie and with the candles lit.

Everyone sings "Happy Birthday" as Nick captures the moment on video. Julie is overwhelmed with such joy. She cries as they sing and looks over at Nick standing next to her. She touches his face with her hand and then looks back at her friends' happy faces.

She makes a wish, the wish that her heart most wants to come true, and blows out all of the candles. Everyone cheers.

The waiter cuts the cake and serves it with vanilla ice cream, just the way Julie loves it. It tastes delicious. "This is the best cake I've ever had, Nick!" she says as she indulges in a piece of birthday cake. "I love it!"

"I'm so glad."

Following cake, she opens thoughtful presents from her friends and thanks them all for being there to celebrate her special day. "It means the world that you're here with me tonight. Thank you for helping to make this my best birthday ever!"

As the waiter cleans up the last bit of confetti and the last guest leaves, Julie kicks off her sparkly gold heels and sits on the dining room table. Nick has been tidying up. He comes over to her with his phone to get a selfie with the birthday girl. They take a few fun shots. He puts a little icing on his finger and playfully dabs it on her face. He takes a few pictures and then kisses it off of her cheek in a selfie. They both laugh, intoxicated by the night's pleasures.

Getting serious for a moment, she says, "This was the most magical night of my life. Thank you."

Now standing and facing her while she sits on the table, Nick says, "It makes me so happy to see you happy." He gives her a quick smooch on her nose.

"What time is it?" she asks, concerned.

He checks his phone. "It's two in the morning."

"It's so late." She takes his hands loosely in hers and looks up into his beautiful blue eyes. Her voice cracks a little as she says, "Stay with me tonight." She seductively slides his suit jacket off of his shoulders.

He looks into her bright green eyes and takes a deep breath.

"Okay."

She lays his jacket across the back of a dining room chair while maintaining eye contact with him. They stare into each other's eyes gently and yet intensely. Time seems to stop completely as they drift into a frozen state that's both still and very active at the same time.

He lightly trails his fingers along her shoulder. With a low voice, he asks, "What was your favorite part of today?"

She slips herself off of the table and stands in front of him. "This moment." She runs her hand through his thick, dark hair. He closes his eyes and exhales audibly. His hair feels so good between her fingers, soft and smooth. Feeling her hands touch him in a new way is a tantalizing experience for him.

"Are you still buzzed from the champagne?" he asks playfully.

"No, I didn't drink very much tonight. I wanted to remember it all. I'm completely sober . . . but I feel drunk on life after this amazing day." She laughs. "How about you?"

"I'm glad to hear that. I only had two glasses much earlier in the evening." He smiles.

He reaches up and plays with one of her dangly gold earrings, admiring its sparkle as well as Julie's own glow. The music stops. They stand in silence, breathing in unison and both wondering if the other can hear their heart beating out loud so hard and fast.

He slowly traces the outline of her eyebrow with his thumb, studying the details of her beautiful face. She closes her eyes and enjoys the sensations of being seen and felt in such a sensual way. She's in a blissful state of not thinking, just being and feeling.

It's getting intense for both of them. Nick opens his mouth to say something to break the tension. She follows her instincts and puts her finger over his mouth to stop him. He smiles a little while trying to read her eyes. She continues looking into his eyes and gently nods her head.

He takes a deep breath. She takes his hand in hers and leads them into her bedroom. He follows her, watching the curve of her body in that purple dress, the way her hips swish as she walks, and every nuanced, feminine move she makes.

She turns to face him again and puts her arms around him. He embraces her, and she can feel his hardness pressing against her through his pants. At first he tries to move his pelvis away so she won't notice, but she pulls him closer to show him it's okay. She's incredibly turned on by this closeness.

She feels a moment of fear but then decides to be brave. She steps away from him and slowly pulls the straps of her dress down around her shoulders. Looking into his eyes, and revealing her beautiful curves, she seductively pushes her dress down to the floor. She stands vulnerably in front of him in just her bra and panties.

Nick is in a trance, lost in her beauty and in her vulnerability. He looks at the detailing on her lingerie, bright pink embroidery on black lace. He runs his hand through his hair, not knowing exactly what to do next. This whole time he's been trying to resist wanting her so badly, and now it's rising to a boil.

Just a foot in front of Nick, she unhooks her bra and holds it loosely, covering her breasts. She moves closer to him. He takes her in his arms and feels the heat from her bare back against his moist palms.

He's imagined this moment so many times. She aches for him, too, and he can feel it. Sensing her desire, he kisses her cheek in a very prolonged, sensual way. She can smell him, and it makes her want him even more. He kisses her face and presses his lips gently against hers for the first time. They look into each other's eyes. She breathes in as he breathes out.

He plays with her hair and pulls her closer to him. They both close their eyes. His tongue plunges into her mouth like a wild animal seeking refuge from a storm. Her heart races as their tongues touch, explore, and caress each other's mouths for the first time.

Sparks are flying beyond what either them have ever felt before. Their chemistry is intense and overwhelming. He pulls away for a moment to look at her, catch his breath, and to check in to make sure that she's all right with all of this.

When he looks into her eyes, they both smile with happy recognition and relief. She unbuttons the top button on his shirt and runs her hands over the back of his pants, feeling the roundness of his firm ass.

He tugs the strap on her bra, pulling it away from her body and onto the floor. He gently pulls her to him and drops to his knees. His strong, sexy hands encapsulate and caress her breasts. "God, you're so beautiful, Julie."

They're both breathing heavily as he licks and playfully sucks her nipples. She releases her head back in complete pleasure.

She feels so alive. He puts his hands around her waist and stands up to kiss her lips again.

He lifts her up and turns to lay her down gently on the bed. "Is this okay?" he asks in a whisper. She nods her head. He kisses her neck and nuzzles her ear with his nose. She tugs at the buttons on his shirt.

Standing up next to the bed, he unbuttons the rest of his shirt seductively. She gives him a sexy grin, enjoying his showmanship.

He pulls his shirt off, revealing his hot body. His strong and sexy body tantalizes her. She loves looking at his muscular chest and chiseled abs. "You're so sexy!" she purrs. Feeling incredibly turned on, she motions for him to come lie next to her on the bed. He obeys.

She pulls his hand for him to roll over on top of her. He looks down at her black lacy panties and kisses her stomach. His mouth sensuously moves from her stomach up to her mouth again while his fingers play along the inside of the lacy band at the top of her panties.

He stops kissing for a moment to catch his breath. He smiles and he admires the bright light reflecting from her eyes. Just when she starts to relax, he plunges his fingers down into her panties and explores her most forbidden area.

She gasps in shock and pleasure. He watches her and responds intuitively to her movements. He smiles at her and sensually kisses her neck as her body writhes in total ecstasy while he touches her.

When he senses that she's about ready to burst, he kisses her mouth passionately and then pulls her panties down and tantalizes her body with his tongue. One hand firmly holds her hip while the other continues delivering delicious pleasure.

She moans loudly and repeatedly, blissfully out of control of her thrashing body while experiencing wave after wave of indulgence. Nick continues the pressure until she climaxes. He lovingly kisses her body and then lies down to rest while admiring her with his eyes.

"That was amazing!" she says while catching her breath.

"*You* are amazing."

Julie can hardly believe that she just had that experience. It was her first time reaching orgasm orally with a man, and it was so easy with him. The way he touched her . . . it was as if he was divinely inspired and knew exactly what to do and the perfect time to do it.

She reaches for him and finds the button and zipper on his pants. Looking into his eyes as if to seek permission, she undoes them. Understanding what she wants, he stands up and slowly lowers his pants, revealing his sexiness wrapped up in a pair of navy blue boxer briefs.

He teases her a little by playing with the waistband. After a few minutes of having fun, pretending he was going to pull them down and then not, he dramatically drops his boxers and reveals himself to her. She gasps. His body is gorgeous, with strong muscle definition and a well groomed, lean physique.

Sweating, she looks at him pleadingly and spreads her legs open on the bed. She can hardly believe her ears when she hears herself say, "I want to feel you inside me. Make love to me."

He smiles as he climbs onto the bed. "Your wish is my command," he says in his sexiest voice and kisses her between her legs. He smooches her stomach, blows on her breasts, licks her collarbone, sucks her neck, nibbles her ear, and finally frenches her mouth as his fingers explore their new territory again.

She reaches for him. Her hands feel his hardness from the thick tip to the long shaft underneath. "Unh . . ." he groans as she touches him.

She can barely take it anymore. She wants to feel him inside of her so bad. He looks into her eyes as if to ask if it's okay to take her now. Her eyes light up and she smiles slightly. "I'll be right back," he whispers.

He gets out of bed and goes into the kitchen to find his wallet in his jacket pocket. He comes back with a condom. He gets into position between her legs and rolls the condom on over his extreme sexiness.

She wants him so badly that it's all she can do to keep from panting and begging. But she knows deep down that Nick would never make her beg. He touches her again, his soft, strong fingers against her wet skin.

Staring into her eyes, he lines himself up to enter her. He comes closer, balancing on his elbows so he can kiss her and feel her body against his.

Looking into his eyes, she wraps her legs around him as he plunges himself inside her wetness. They both moan loudly at the feeling of being so close to each other. It's the best sensation she's ever experienced. For a moment he pauses inside her and they both gasp in pleasure as he kisses her passionately.

Slowly, he goes deeper and faster, moaning and watching the pleasure on her face.

He slows down a little and then speeds up again. His fingers play with her while she enjoys his thrusts. Her body pulls him inside her and she cums again, shaking in pleasure. He kisses her and continues making love to her with his body, his eyes, and his soul. She feels a deep fusion with him, unlike anything she's ever felt during sex before.

She feels him tense up and sees in his eyes that's he's about to explode inside her. She grabs his ass and pulls him toward her even harder. He holds his breath for a moment and then releases a massive moan as he climaxes.

Holding her, he kisses her chin and suckles her neck seductively. He wraps his arms around her back and gently rolls so that he's on his back and she's lying on top of him, still with him inside.

Leaning down to kiss his chest, his sweat tastes both salty and sweet. It feels cool against her hot skin. She hears and feels his heart beating loudly against her cheek. She closes her eyes, and she is calm, euphoric, and whole.

As they both catch their breath, Nick feels the ecstasy of being with her in this new, more intimate way. He picks her hand up and brings it to his mouth for a kiss. "I love you so much, Julie," he whispers in her ear and kisses her forehead.

"I love you, too."

Thirty

Sun shines in through the crease in the curtains as Julie awakens naked in bed next to the sexiest man she's ever known. She lies there for a moment, calmed by the rhythm of Nick's breathing, yet she is also anxious.

Nick spoons her, holding her in his strong arms. She feels the warmth of his skin against her body. He lightly shifts her hair away from her back and kisses her neck and shoulders, and romantically purrs, "Good morning, sexy!"

She rolls over to see his handsome face. "Morning!" She smiles as he smooches her on the lips.

"What time is your event today?" he asks while stroking her cheek.

She thinks for a moment. "I'm on stage at 4 p.m. and signing afterward until 7."

"Making love to you last night was one of the most incredible experiences I've ever had . . ." he starts to speak but then stops. "I know you're afraid, Julie. I can see it in your eyes and feel it in your energy."

He kisses her tenderly on her lips and then on her forehead. She looks at him with a tremendous vulnerability shining through.

He continues, "It's okay. I'm not those other guys. I just want to love, cherish, protect, and pleasure you. I would never hurt you. Your heart is safe with me."

She looks up at him, teary-eyed. She gently puts her arms around his neck, smiles, and pushes her lips against his. He kisses her passionately.

"I have a hopeful heart, Nick. If I ever lost you from my life . . ."

"I'm the happiest man in the world to wake up next to you. You are so precious. I'd risk everything to be with you. I want to make you deliriously happy." He smiles and kisses the tip of her nose.

She smiles. "I like that. I want us both to be deliriously happy."

"Mission accomplished." He takes her face in his hands and leans in for a passionate kiss that takes her breath away.

He stops abruptly. They both breathe heavily. "I love you, Julie. I've been in love with you for so long. I was afraid to tell you, to admit that this was the real deal. You make me feel the most alive I've ever felt. I'm not afraid anymore. I want you in my life. You are worth every risk. I'll do anything, whatever it takes to be your man."

She smiles, holding back happy tears.

"How on earth did I make it so long being close to you and not kissing you? You're irresistible!" He kisses her neck playfully, pretending to bite her.

She laughs. "I was just wondering the same thing. Your smell is intoxicating. I can't keep my eyes or my hands off of you. How am I ever going to get out of bed to go to my event today?"

"How about I go with you? That'll make it easier."

Julie finishes up on stage and is thrilled to receive a standing ovation. She takes a quick break to the ladies room with the help of Jackson, the big and buff bodyguard that's been assigned to her for the day.

Returning to her signing table, she's greeted by a mob of excited fans. They cheer as they see her approaching. She hopes all this love from her readers never gets old.

She's hugging, hearing stories, taking pictures, and signing books for hours. At one point she sees Nick stop by out of the corner of her eye. He smiles and waves to her. A few minutes later he comes by the table and gives her a cool bottle of water.

"Oh, thank you, Nick," she says with relief.

"Great turnout today, huh?"

"Wonderful! I may be a little later than I planned." She smiles apologetically.

"Absolutely understand. Text me if you need anything." He squeezes her shoulder and then walks away.

A few minutes later, glancing up at the line, she sees a familiar form appear at the end. Large, cartoon-like, and wearing his signature smirk, she sees Will waiting in her line. *Oh no.* She sends a quick text to Nick: "Will is here."

She focuses on making conversation with each fan and distracts herself until he's next in line.

When he reaches her, she looks him right in the eyes and quietly but firmly says, "Go away, Will."

"Wait—I want to talk with you."

Keeping her voice down so no one else will hear, she says, "No, I'm done talking with you. I'm working. Go away."

He doesn't budge. "The least you could do is hear me out."

"You're being disrespectful and disrupting my event. Please leave me alone. I'm calling security now," she says, turning to Jackson.

"Is this because I didn't call you for a few months? You're overreacting."

"Security!" she yells.

Jackson walks over and asks Will to leave quietly. "Do you see that tiny, sexy woman over there?" he says, pointing at Julie as he leads him away.

"Yeah."

"My job is to keep creeps like you away from her so she can do her job."

They start to argue. During their confrontation, Nick approaches them.

"Oh, I guess now her assistant is going to escort me out of the building," he says with attitude toward Nick.

Nick keeps his voice low and says, "Look, you're being a douche. If you really want to talk with her, call her after her event." Jackson physically escorts him further away from the table.

Julie goes back to focusing on her readers now that she knows the Will situation is in good hands.

"You don't know anything," Will spits at Nick.

"I know that a real man wouldn't exploit someone he cared about, selling those photos. I know that a real man wouldn't trick a woman into thinking he had feelings for her to get her into bed. And, a real man would be respectful and have an adult conversation before he disappeared."

"I could kick your ass!" yells Will. Jackson moves his formidable body between the two of them.

Nick feels exasperated. "I'm not sure what that would accomplish."

"I'm in love with her, okay?" Will blurts out, shocked at the words coming out of his own mouth.

Nick looks at him incredulously. "What are you talking about?"

Will looks down at the ground for a moment and then over Nick's shoulder. "I don't know. Something is happening to me that I don't understand. I have feelings for her that I haven't felt before. I just want to talk with her."

Trying to stay calm, Nick says, "Whoa . . . that's big, but now's not the time."

"Will you ask her to call me and tell her it's important?"

Nick hesitates. "Fine."

Will breathes a sigh of relief. "Thanks, man." He walks away.

Jackson shrugs his massive shoulders and shakes his head. "Didn't see that coming."

"Me neither," Nick says.

Thirty-one

"So, how did it go today?" asks Nick as he helps Julie load her boxes into his truck.

"It was great, I had fun. And it was a record-breaking day for me," she says with exhaustion in her voice.

"That's great." He pauses for a moment as he loads the last box. "So what happened with Will?" He walks over to face her eye-to-eye and holds her hands.

"I saw him there and freaked out. I was so hurt by him and so angry about the photos. It all came flooding back to me. Even though everything worked out okay, I didn't want to talk to him."

Nick says, "I understand. I told him he was being a douche."

"Totally. Thanks for getting him to leave."

"I think Jackson was the primary motivator for that," he jokes.

"He was pretty badass, huh?" She giggles. "I thought Will was built until I saw him next to Jackson . . . Will could've been his mini-me." They both laugh.

"He really wants you to call him. He asked me to tell you," he says calmly.

"Yeah, that's not going to happen. He's so weird."

"He told me something interesting once he calmed down." Julie looks at him quizzically. "He said that he's in love with you."

"What? That guy must be crazy."

Standing in front of her, looking into her eyes, Nick says, "Crazy about you." He rubs her shoulders.

"Ooh, that feels really good," she says while closing her eyes and tilting her head back a little.

"He's not the only one, you know?" says Nick with a smile. She opens her eyes and appreciates his handsome face.

"Really?" she asks playfully. "Tell me more."

Just then a group of teenagers approaches them. Several girls start giggling nervously and come over to Julie and ask for a photo. "Sure," she agrees.

Nick takes their picture in the parking lot and they all happily hug Julie and scamper off.

"I guess we should go before your location is revealed and the paparazzi find us," Nick jokes as he opens the passenger door for her.

She laughs and gets into the truck.

He puts his hand on her leg. "You did an amazing job today. I'm really proud of you. Glad I got to see you in action." He smiles.

"Thank you, I'm happy you were here. I appreciate all of your help."

He leans over to kiss her lightly on her mouth. "I've missed your luscious lips today."

She smiles and returns his kiss.

Her phone rings mid-kiss. She pulls it from her purse to find that Will is calling. She shows it to Nick, who's starting the truck, then sends it directly to voicemail.

Changing the subject, she asks, "Maybe we could eat in tonight?"

"There's a great Indian restaurant on the way to your place. We could get take out if you want." He looks over at her longingly.

"That sounds perfect."

They're both quiet for a minute. Nick breaks the silence by asking, "Are you going to call him back?"

"Will? Why?"

"Uh, um . . . I was just wondering . . ." he says almost apologetically.

"No, I didn't mean it that way. I meant, why would I? I don't have anything to say to him, and I'm not dropping everything that matters in my life just because he's decided that he wants to talk to me."

She pulls out her phone and blocks his number.

Nick looks relieved. "I love a strong woman," he says with a wink.

A few days later, Julie finishes up hip-hop class and is sweaty in her leopard print sport leggings and racer-back tank top. They learned a sexy new dance, and she's exhausted and ready for a shower. As she walks toward the door, she sees an unexpected and familiar face through the glass walls.

Waiting just beyond the door is Will. *Ugh.* She realizes that there's no escape from interacting with him. He's blocking the only exit. She says goodbye to her friends and pulls over to the side of the room for a moment to text Nick. "Will is outside of my studio blocking my exit."

She walks through the door and looks straight at him. He immediately approaches her with a hug. She doesn't hug him back and doesn't stand still for long.

"Hey Julie. It's so good to see you and your sexy self. Damn . . . you looked so hot dancing in there," says Will.

"How long have you been here?" she asks, incredulous.

"I don't know, maybe 45 minutes. I knew you had dance class on Wednesday nights, so I figured that this would be the only way to talk to you since you're not returning my calls."

She continues walking. "I don't have anything else to talk with you about, Will. And I'm uncomfortable with you being here right now. Please leave me alone."

Will ignores her request. "I just waited all this time to talk to you and you're going to walk away?"

"That's right. I don't owe you anything." She dabs her face and neck with a towel. Her hair is soaked, so she undoes her ponytail to let it dry faster.

He grabs her shoulder. "Hey, let's just talk for a few minutes . . . please?"

She moves away from him and calmly tells him, "Don't touch me."

"I just want to talk to you. Please." He drops down to his knees and pretends to beg her. People are starting to stare.

"I need to get home, Will. It's been a long day, and I'm tired. I don't have time for this," she says compassionately but firmly.

He makes a pouty face and whimpers like a dog.

"Please stop that. You can't manipulate me anymore."

He looks annoyed and stands up. "I just need to tell you a few things."

"Not tonight, I gotta go." She opens the studio door to the parking lot. He follows her to her car.

"Look, when you said goodbye to me that day so easily, it made me wonder where your head was at. And then when you said we couldn't be friends, I thought that was ridiculous. But I missed you. I've never had a woman completely cut me out of her life before. I didn't like it."

She looks at him. "What's your point?"

"I realized that you make me a better man. I actually like who I am when I'm around you. I could use more of that in my life. You're so beautiful, and smart, and . . . incredible in bed. I don't know what I was thinking that day. I guess I just got scared."

"I don't think so. Now I really need to go," she says as she opens her car door. He holds the door open, preventing her from closing it.

"I love you. There, I said it. I've never said it to anyone before."

"Do you even hear yourself? You used me to work at your event, dumped me right before you were supposed to meet my family, sold terrible paparazzi-style photos of me to the media, didn't talk to me for months, and now it's all about you. You haven't even apologized for what you did or asked how I am or anything about me at all. Do you realize how selfish you are?"

Her phone rings. It's Nick calling. "Leave me alone, Will. You don't love me. You're in love with yourself and with having someone around to worship you. I'm not that girl anymore, and I never will be."

She answers her phone as she attempts to close the car door. Will refuses to move. "Hello?"

"Are you okay?"

"Sort of."

"Is he there right now?"

"Yes, unfortunately."

"I'm almost at the studio. I'll find you."

"Thank you," she says, hanging up the phone to find Will has wedged himself between the car and the driver's side door.

She looks up at him. "I have nothing more to say, Will. You're wasting both of our time."

"But I told you I love you." His expression twists itself into a knot as his face reddens.

"I told you that I need to leave, and you're disrespecting my wishes yet again."

He leans forward inside the car and attempts to kiss her on the mouth.

She pushes him away as he struggles to overcome her. "Come on, Julie, just one kiss."

He pushes his body into her with full force and grabs tightly a hold of her left wrist. "Get off of me! Stop it!" She slams on the horn as she attempts to push him out of the door.

She's struggling to get Will's hands and lips away from her. He's much bigger and stronger than she is and is using it to his advantage. His tongue sloppily invades her mouth as she bites down hard.

Suddenly she feels relief as he's pulled away from her and the car. She's finally able to shut her door.

She looks over to see that Nick has grabbed Will by the shoulders and knocked him onto the ground on the grassy median in the parking lot.

"What the fuck are you doing, Will?" he shouts and restrains him. His heart is pumping a mile a minute and the adrenaline is giving him superhuman strength.

"None of your business."

"You can't go around stalking Julie and forcing yourself on her. You need to leave her alone," Nick commands.

Will is quiet for a moment while catching his breath. "I thought you were going to tell her to call me."

"She's a free woman and can call or not call anyone she wants. Just because you want to talk to her all of a sudden doesn't mean she wants to talk to you."

"Whatever." He seems calmer now so Nick stands up and allows him to get up off of the ground but stays between him and the car.

Will looks over at Julie sitting in her car looking at him angrily. "This is not what I wanted. I hope you're happy," he says with a snarl and walks away.

Nick watches him for a minute until he's sure that he's actually leaving and then turns to Julie. He opens her car door. "Oh my God, are you okay?"

She slowly nods. She's a little shaken from Will's surprising aggressiveness.

"Here, let me drive you home," he says as he offers her his hand to help her out of the car and into the passenger seat.

She steps out and hugs him tightly. "But what about your truck?"

"I'll just leave it here in the lot, and I'll get a cab back once I'm sure that you're safe." He leads her around the car and opens the door for her.

She's quiet the entire drive home. He reaches over and offers his hand for her to hold. She interlaces her fingers in his. He looks down and notices a bruise forming in the shape of Will's handprint on her wrist and realizes how scary that experience must've been for Julie. He respects her silence. He drives to her place and when they arrive, he walks her inside.

Once they get inside, she starts the water running for a shower. He puts some relaxing music on for her in the bathroom and kisses her forehead. "I'll get some dinner going for us. I'm right here if you need me."

She nods and closes the bathroom door when he leaves.

When she emerges from the shower, Nick is sitting in her kitchen responding to an email on his phone. He looks up to see her with her wet hair and fluffy bathrobe. He puts his phone down on the table and walks over to her.

"How are you feeling?" he says as he holds her.

"Better. A little confused."

"Let's sit down and talk while we eat."

She walks into the bedroom and props some pillows up for each of them along the headboard. He brings two plates of spaghetti with shrimp into the bedroom for them.

"Thank you for showing up for me tonight," she says as she accepts her plate.

"My pleasure," he says as he digs in.

"I still don't know what happened. It escalated so fast," she says, staring off at the wall.

He touches her leg reassuringly. "It's okay. You did the right things by telling him no, texting me, pushing him away, and blaring your horn. That's how I found you so quickly."

"He was so grabby, pulling on my arms, putting his mouth on my face, trying to touch me. It was disgusting. But he was so strong, I couldn't get him off of me. I felt like I couldn't breathe." She touches the tender spot on her wrist where Will held onto her so tightly.

"That must have been terrifying," he says. "Thank God you texted me and answered your phone."

He lightly picks up her left hand and gently kisses the bruised area all around her wrist. "I'm going to get you some ice for your wrist," he says as he heads back into the kitchen.

Big tears start rolling down her cheeks and onto her dinner plate. "I was really scared, Nick. I didn't want to show it, but he shocked me. I've never had anyone kiss me against my will. I just want him to leave me alone."

He wraps a bag of frozen lima beans in a kitchen towel around her wrist and then puts his arms around her as she lays her head on his shoulder. "It's okay. You didn't do anything wrong. He's an asshole." He rubs her arm.

"When I came around the corner and saw him forcing himself on you, something almost snapped within me. I was so angry that I was concerned that I might actually get into a fight with him once I pulled him off of you." She looks up at him. "I love you so much, Julie, and I won't let anyone hurt you."

She finishes the last bite of shrimp, lies down, and pulls him over to lie with her. He holds her and kisses her forehead. She looks up at him through watery eyes. "Why are you so good to me, Nick?"

He looks surprised. "What do you mean?"

"Well, you've always been so different than other guys."

"I can't help but be good to you. I love you. I guess in some way I always have." He looks at her lovingly. "And, unfortunately, the guys you've dated have been boys, not men. You deserve to be treated well by a real man."

She snuggles her head under his chin and runs her hand along the muscular indentation in his stomach. She says suddenly, "I'm thinking about going to Europe for a few weeks."

"Oh? Business or pleasure?"

"A little bit of both. Today I got a call from a friend in Paris offering to take me on private tours of castles and wineries in the French countryside."

"Wow! That sounds amazing!" He caresses her shoulder.

"I think it would be good research and inspiration for the novel I'm writing now. And, it's been a little crazy here in the U.S. lately since those pictures went viral," she laughs and props her head up on her bent arm, looking into his eyes.

"That sounds like it could be a great trip."

"My friend said I could use his frequent flier miles, and that it would be a treat to have me there. I could make a lot of progress on my novel. So I'm thinking about leaving in a week while I have time between speaking engagements."

"Cool. How long will you be gone?" he asks calmly, trying to remain supportive while thinking about how much he'll miss her while she's away.

"I'm not sure . . . probably two to three weeks."

He shifts his body so that he's sitting up and leaning on his arm. "Do you think you'd travel alone?"

"Yes, for the most part. I would stay with my friend and his family in France and travel with them through the countryside."

"Well, I'll definitely miss you while you're traveling, but you have my full support. I know Paris is your favorite city in the world. What a great opportunity to go! Let me know what I can do to help. I can take you to the airport, check up on your house while you're away, whatever you need."

"Thank you, Nick. I'll let you know what I decide to do."

He leans forward to lightly touch his lips to hers. "Is this okay?" he asks realizing that she may not want to kiss anyone after the experience she had earlier. She receives his kiss and gently kisses him back. "Do you want me to stay tonight?" he whispers.

"I'd love for you to stay."

Thirty-two

"I can't believe you'll be gone for three whole weeks!" Nick says as he loads Julie's suitcases into his truck.

"I know, I'm excited for my trip but I'm trying not to think about it."

He closes her door and walks around to the driver's seat. "Do you have everything?"

She looks back at her luggage and says, "I think so. I guess I'm ready." She smiles.

Nick fumbles for something in his pocket and pulls out a small blue box with a white bow. "I got you a little going away present."

He looks nervous as he hands it to her. "Oh my God, Nick! You are so amazing!" she says as she excitedly removes the white bow to reveal "Tiffany & Company" on the lid of the box.

"I've never had anything from Tiffany's before," she says looking up at him with anticipation.

He smiles. "I know. I thought it was time for that to change."

She lifts the lid from the box and pulls out a velvet drawstring bag with the brand embroidered across it. Carefully opening the little bag, she pulls a delicate silver chain featuring an Eiffel Tower pendant. She gasps with joy. "I love it!"

She unbuckles her seatbelt and climbs over into Nick's lap in the driver's seat. "You are so thoughtful. Thank you for this beautiful gift!" She kisses him passionately as he holds her in his arms.

She puts the pendant on around her neck and hugs him again before climbing back into her seat.

"I'm glad you like it. I wanted to give you something that would make you smile each day while you're away." He starts the truck and drives her to the airport.

"I don't know how much Internet or phone access I'll have while I'm there," she says apologetically. "I'm really going to miss you. I'll try to keep in touch as much as I can."

He pats her leg and then holds her hand. "It's okay, I understand. You're there to work on your novel—I know how important that is to you." He pauses for a moment in thought. "I guarantee that I'll be thinking of you every day . . . and remembering our romantic morning." He winks at her.

She laughs. "Yes, I'm sure I'll be thinking about that often." He laughs with her and kisses her hand.

"What day are you back?" he asks.

"On the twenty-second. My mom is picking me up."

When they arrive at the airport, they park and he carries her bags inside to the counter for her. He walks with her as far as he can until he can go no further. He gives her a passionate kiss and touches her face. "I'm memorizing you," he says with a chuckle. She detects some sadness in his voice.

"Don't worry, you're unforgettable." She kisses him once more and then walks through the security line. He waits and watches her. When she gets ready to go through the metal detector, she turns around, meets eyes with him, and blows him a kiss. He smiles and blows her a kiss back, then watches her walk out of sight.

Nick and Asa are working out the in gym. "So, how are you holding up?" Asa asks teasingly.

"Honestly, man, it's not easy being away from her this long without being able to communicate with her."

"Have you tried to call her?" Asa asks as he does pushups.

"Yeah, I left her a voicemail on her first day away, but I don't think her phone is working because I didn't hear back from her." They trade places. "I haven't seen any online updates, so I don't think she has Internet access either."

"Well, she'll be back in another week," he responds while setting up the weight machine.

Nick is on the ground doing pushups. "I miss everything about her . . . her smile, her voice, her laugh, her eyes, her body, even just talking with her."

Asa finishes his set. "I've never seen you like this before, Nick. Sounds like someone is in love."

Nick smiles. "I've never felt this way before about anyone or anything in my life. It's crazy. I'm daydreaming about living together and starting a family with her."

"Whoa . . . that is deep!" says Asa as he takes Nick's place on the weight machines.

Back on the floor for pushups, Nick says, "I've been thinking about asking her to marry me."

"Don't you think you should ask her to be your girlfriend first?" laughs Asa.

"I guess I just assumed that she already was my girlfriend," he says with chagrin.

"Do you think that she thinks of you more as her best friend or her boyfriend?"

Nick thinks for a moment. "I have no idea. I've never thought about like that. We didn't talk about being exclusive, but she knows that I'm in love with her." He sits on the weight bench and wiping the sweat from his face.

An extremely attractive woman comes over, sits down on the weight bench next to Nick, and starts to chat with him. Twirling her hair and leaning over strategically so he could see her cleavage, he doesn't seem to notice at all. Instead, he asks her, "Can I get your opinion on something from a woman's perspective?"

Thinking that he's going to ask her out in some clever way, she says, "Sure."

He then asks her how long it takes for a woman to think of a man she's dating as her boyfriend. The woman giggles and seductively says, "You can be my boyfriend right now."

Asa laughs.

"What?" asks Nick as if waking up from a dream. "No, that's not what I meant. Sorry." He gets up and walks over to a different machine. It's as if that conversation never happened.

"Do you think she's seeing other guys while she's traveling?" he asks Asa.

"That doesn't seem like her style . . . but, if you guys haven't talked about being in an exclusive relationship . . ."

Nick looks at him and thinks it over. "Damn, you're right," he says. "It's so hard being away from her. I can't wait to see her on the twenty-second."

"Are you picking her up from the airport?" asks Asa.

"No, her mom is planning to be there . . . but maybe I can surprise her?" Nick says with excitement in his voice.

As the plane touches down at LAX airport, Julie turns her phone on for the first time in three weeks, receiving all of her texts, emails, online messages, and voicemails in a flurry. She's overwhelmed with the volume of them and decides to take care of them later. *It's been three weeks already, what's another day or two?*

She texts her mom, letting her know she's arrived, and gives her the baggage claim number. Then she texts Nick, the man she's been thinking about nonstop since the moment she left—what seems like years ago. "Hey Nick! Just landed at LAX. Missed you. See you soon!"

Thinking about seeing him again has her feeling excited and nervous. Her skin breaks out in goose bumps just imagining it. She hopes that he's been thinking of her as much as she's been thinking of him, but she tries to tell herself that everything will be okay if things aren't the way she hopes. She's not sure what to expect.

Nick hears the happy tweet of his phone and looks down to see his first text from Julie since she left. He smiles, knowing that she's safe back in the U.S. and that she's thinking of him. He has been worried that he wasn't clear enough about his feelings for her before she left. He hopes that he still has a chance with the most amazing woman he's ever known.

Julie comes through the International Arrivals gate on her way to baggage claim. After traveling throughout France for three weeks, she's tired and happy to be back in the U.S. She loves to travel, and is always grateful to sleep in her own bed when she returns.

As she makes her way around the corner, she's shocked to see Nick standing there, dressed in a suit and holding at least two dozen long-stemmed red roses in his arms. He doesn't see her at first, and she studies him. He looks incredibly handsome, even more than she remembers, and also a little nervous.

Their eyes meet, and he gets a giant smile across his face and moves toward her. Not sure what he's doing there, but so happy to see him, she runs to him and throws her arms around him.

"Julie, I missed you so much," he says holding her in his arms for the first time in what feels like an eternity. "God, you look amazing. How are you? How was your trip?" he asks, taking it all in.

She smiles, still hugging him. "I had an incredible trip. It was life changing. And, I finished writing my book."

"That's wonderful, Julie. I'm so happy to hear that."

He takes a deep breath. "I have a bold confession," he says. "I want to be your everything, to go to bed at night together and to wake up with you in my arms. I want to kiss you passionately every day and feel your beautiful body against mine every night. I want to know what you're thinking and feeling. I want to have adventures with you. I love your courage and your confidence, the way you go for what you want in life. I love your intensity and your excitement about things. I even love your face when you cry. You deserve a real man who puts you first. You are incredibly special and I can't imagine living my life without you in it."

Nick takes another deep breath, looks at her and kisses her forehead, then continues.

"I've been doing a lot of thinking while you've been away. Oh Julie, I yearn to be with you, to spend time with you – even if it's just running errands or going to the gym. I light up whenever you're around. At first I thought it was because of our close friendship, but now I know it's much more. When I look at you, my heart smiles and jumps a little in my chest. I think about you all the time and can't wait to find out how your day went.

"I realized that I can't wait to see you and it doesn't matter when or where, I'll do whatever it takes to be with you, even for just a few minutes. I have deep feelings for you that go way beyond friendship and beyond anything I've felt before with anyone else. I can't imagine my life without you in it."

Julie is taken aback by everything she's hearing. She feels dizzy, like she's in a dream. She smiles and gets ready to speak. Nick says, "I've been waiting for so long to work up the courage to tell you how I feel. Please, just let me pour my soul out to you . . ."

Nick takes another deep breath, kisses her hand, and continues, "You're the most beautiful, loving, sexy, and amazing woman I've ever had the privilege to know. I feel the most alive when we're together—no matter whether we're laughing, crying, or just talking."

Julie looks into his beautiful eyes and enjoys their sparkle. Nick says, "When you spent that night with Will, it about drove me crazy. I had no idea at the time why it affected me so strongly. Now I realize that it awakened my deep feelings for you. I'm so in love with you, Jules."

Nick pauses and takes another deep breath. He musters up his courage and continues, "I'm nervous to tell you all of this, but I'm more afraid of not telling you and never getting the chance to be your man. So, there it is . . . all my heart and soul before you. How are you feeling?"

Just then the crowd that's gathered around them witnessing this beautiful love scene breaks into applause and cheers. Nick and Julie are oblivious to anything but each other.

Nick looks nervously at Julie's face for any sign of a reaction. Julie is stunned and stares at him for a minute before responding. "Oh my God, Nick. I'm floored. You've been my best friend for so long, and I've tried not to think of you in that way because of our friendship. I was so scared of losing you as my closest friend." Nick looks disappointed but tries to listen and understand.

Julie sees his disappointment and hugs him tighter. "But, if I'm completely honest, I've always had a thing for you. You're the best man I've ever known, and we're really good together."

Nick looks relieved. "Would you do me the honor of being my girlfriend? I really want to do things right with you and treat you the way you truly deserve to be treated."

"I would love to! But, there's just one thing we need to do first."

"What?" Nick asks, not sure what to expect.

"Kiss."

Nick steps closer to Julie and gently touches her face with his hand. He looks deep into her eyes. She sees his twinkly blue eyes gently close as he leans his body into hers and brushes his soft, moist lips against hers for the first time in weeks.

The mere touch of Nick's hand and feeling the heat from his body and his breath so close to hers is enough to make her stomach flutter. His sexy smell and exploring eyes melt her right away. Julie leans her lips into his and receives his sensual kiss. She can feel his passion and yearning for her through the movement of his tongue against hers. It's the most beautiful, soulful, and intense kiss she's ever experienced. When it ends, they are both speechless, just staring mesmerized into each other's eyes and gently holding each other for what seems like a never-ending moment of bliss. Julie knows that it's a forever kiss.

The crowd goes wild, but neither of them pays attention to anyone but each other. Time is standing still, and they're the only two people in the universe in this moment. "I missed you. You were right, Nick, all of my dreams *are* coming true!"

Thirty-three

They stop for dinner at a charming Italian restaurant on the way to Julie's home in Malibu. Over the course of the meal, Julie and Nick gaze into each other's eyes, share updates on what's been happening in the last three weeks, and talk about the future.

During dinner, she surprises him with a gift from France, a heavy coffee table book featuring French architecture including many of the castles she toured. Nick loves her thoughtful gift and feels like the luckiest man on the planet to be reunited with his true love. It's the perfect "welcome home" dinner and both leave with their hearts and stomachs full.

"Do you know what today is, Nick?" she asks as he brings her luggage into her home and she puts her roses into a large vase.

"Today would've been your wedding anniversary, right?"

She smiles. "You have a great memory."

"I'm so glad that you are feeling better now. I've missed you so much." He wraps his arms around her from behind while she arranges the flowers.

Feeling him against her turns her on. She turns around and kisses him passionately. "You know what else?" she asks between kisses.

"I'm all ears." He smooches her on the tip of her nose.

She pulls the collar of her shirt down to reveal the dainty silver chain and Eiffel Tower pendant he gave her. He smiles. "I've worn it every day since I left. It made me feel closer to you while I was away."

"Aw, I'm so glad you like it." He squeezes her again.

"What would my hot boyfriend like to do tonight?" she asks playfully.

"Hmm . . . I have a few ideas." He smiles between kisses. "But first, I have a surprise for you!"

"Ooh, another surprise?"

He kisses her forehead. "Go sit on the bed and close your eyes."

"I like it already!" she says and skips into the bedroom.

"Are your eyes closed?" he calls from the kitchen.

"Yes!"

She hears him rustling around in the refrigerator and her silverware drawer. She smells something delicious as he lifts a fork to her mouth. She instinctively opens her mouth and receives a luscious bite of the most sinfully delicious cake she's ever eaten.

"Mmm . . . red velvet," she says. "Wow!"

He leans over to kiss her and she licks the rich buttercream frosting from his lips. "I have some champagne for us, too, if you'd like some."

Cake in Bed

"I'd love some bubbly . . . and more cake!" They both laugh as he feeds her another bite. "You can open your eyes," he says seductively.

He starts to open the champagne, but as he removes the wire cage, the cork pops out on its own and flies up into the air, startling them both. "Wow . . . I've never seen that before," he says. "I guess sometimes the energy builds up inside so much that it's just ready to go."

She watches him as he pours her a glass of champagne and then one for himself. Being in France gave her a lot of time to think about life and love. Looking at Nick with his sparkly eyes, handsome smile, sexy hair, strong body, and masculine hands right in front of her now almost brings tears to her eyes.

To get to be so close to someone she's missed so much is the best feeling in the world. And, to know that he's just as crazy about her . . . her heart is so full.

He looks at her with love shining through his eyes and feeds her another bite of cake.

Julie raises her glass. "To the most extraordinary, loving, and sexy boyfriend I've ever had. You are my wildest dream come true."

They clink glasses and sip. She feeds him a piece of cake and sensually licks the extra frosting from her fingers. Nick smiles and leans in for a kiss.

While holding her, he raises his glass, "Once upon a time there was a beautiful princess who vanquished a dragon and ruled her kingdom with love and grace. One day, she met a prince who vowed to spend the rest of his life making her happy. To love, laughter, and happily ever after."

THE END

Love and Gratitude

I'm overwhelmed with love and gratitude for everyone who believed in me and helped my *Cake in Bed* dream come true!

A heartfelt thanks to my mom for being an incredible role model and my biggest Fan. Thank you for always believing in me and my crazy dreams.

I'm so grateful to my sister for being one of my dearest friends. Your love, support, and friendship mean the world to me.

Many thanks to Ranj for being an amazing friend who inspires me every day.

Thank you to Sandra for being my soul sister and dream-storming partner.

Huge thanks to Winston for sharing your talents and your heart with me. You are a true alchemist.

I'm grateful to my beautiful friends Angie, August, Eve, Jackie, Jolene, Priyanka, Rebecca, and Stephanie for encouraging me to follow my inspiration and cheering me on along the way. I know the best is on the way for each of you and can't wait to celebrate your success!

Thank you to Owen for sharing your pure heart and unconditional love.

I'm grateful to my dad for your encouragement and support.

Huge thanks to the amazing people from around the world who made this book possible: Alice Refauvelet, Amber Allen, Ann Morgan James, April Spaniol, Brenda Everts, Christina Courtney, Cindy Ertman, Connie Hebert, Craig Klein, Dalia Ibarra, Danielle Soucy Mills, Darril Gibson, David Brower, David Laurell, Debra Tischler, Erin, Eva Lisle, Missy Carpenter, Dr. Frances Collier, Francesca Romero, Glen and Fiona Orr, Janet Wiszowaty, Janis Thomas, Jeannett Jackman, Jed Doherty, Jeff Stout, Jennifer Hines, Jody Schwartz, Juliette Willoughby, Karma Christine Salvato, Kathleen Seeley, Kayla Stevenson, Krista Magidson, Kristin Johnson, Lanette Pottle, Laurie Maroni, Leona Flamel, Lucy Ravitch, Maddie Margarita, Madeline Sharples, Maelia Davis, Marie Ohanesian Nardin, Mayra Llado Ortega, Melanie Sergent, Monica, Nina, Raitis Stalazs, Sasha Morello, ShaSha Logadi, Shelby Peterson, Stacy Morgan, Stephen Hobbs, Stephen Kam, Trina Hall, Werner Artinger, William Kim, Zsuzsa Novak

Extra special thanks to extraordinary gentlemen Michael Egan and Brian Hornberger.

A heartfelt thank you to Jack Canfield for empowering me to follow my heart and pursue my passions in life and in business.

Thank you to my editor, Michelle Josette, whose expertise helped bring *Cake in Bed* to life. It was an honor and a joy to work with you.

Cake in Bed

I am grateful to Miguel Garcia for being my go-to graphic design professional.

Thank you to Kelsey at K Keeton Designs for creating a beautiful cover for *Cake in Bed*.

I'm especially grateful to you, the reader, for embarking on this journey with me. Wishing you love, bliss, and many *Cake in Bed* moments!

About the Author

SHERI FINK is a #1 best-selling author, award-winning entrepreneur, and hopeful romantic who lives in Southern California. She was inspired to write *Cake in Bed*, her debut novel, to empower women to be their authentic selves and to not settle for less than they deserve in life or in love, because everyone deserves to have their cake and eat it too . . . preferably in bed!

www.SheriFink.com

Facebook.com/SheriFinkFan

@Sheri_Fink

CPSIA information can be obtained at www.ICGtesting.com
Printed in the USA
LVOW10s1708200916

505435LV00020B/1804/P